Murder On The Menu

Nancy Pflum

Cover design by Katherine Schumm

www.schummwords.com

This is a work of fiction. All characters, locations, and events are either products of the author's imagination or are used fictionally.

ACKNOWLEDGEMENTS

To my family and friends for their encouragement and support.

To my friends in the Writer Wannabees group of The Villages who guided me through this work with invaluable knowledge and skill.

To Katherine Schumm who designed the cover of this book. You are a patient woman!

To my niece, Tammie Krauskopf, thank you for being my first reader. Your suggestions were insightful and very helpful.

To my husband, Tony, who helped me with all my technical problems.

To my husband, Tony. You are my best friend and the love of my life. Thank you for always being there.

Chapter 1

I love living in Shipley, Ohio, and working with Gus, my friend and boss, in his restaurant in the center of town. Our downtown is only four blocks long, but it's charming with its old, stately buildings and a lovely park nearby.

However, four guys have started coming to Gus's Place the past week, and I'm becoming worried. Whoever they are, I've a feeling they're up to no good. The way they watch our every move is unnerving. It's like we're being cased. Gus wants us to treat our customers with respect and be friendly so they keep coming back. Something tells me that's not the reaction we want from this group.

Today they are overstaying their welcome. It's closing time, and they need to move on. I go to their table in the back. "We're closing now. Here's your check, and please pay at the register."

"Go get your boss." The guy who's speaking is a scary dude. He must be around my age, twenty-six or so. He's got an ugly scar running down the left side of his face. His dark hair is on the long side. To me he looks greasy.

I don't know why, but I have a bad feeling about this. I turn and walk back to the kitchen. "Hey, Gus, some customers want to talk to you."

"Is something wrong?" Gus asks putting down a pan he was washing. He wipes his hands on a towel.

"I don't know. They just asked for you. "

1

Gus frowns at me, then goes out to see them. I watch from the food window. Once he leaves the kitchen, I see him straighten up. Gus is sixty years old, but he still makes an imposing presentation due to his six foot height. Not like me at five foot two.

Gus reaches the table. "I'm Gus Breckman, the owner. You wanted to see me?"

"Yeah, old man, there's a problem. You haven't been paying your taxes."

Scar Face, my name for him, is doing the talking. The other three group members are silent but look tough. They're the kind I wouldn't want to run into in a dark alley.

Gus shakes his head. "What are you talking about? My accountant handles all that. My taxes are up to date."

"That's the feds. I'm talking about your protection money."

"Protection? Like insurance? I have that, too."

I see Scar Face roll his eyes. "Got a slow one here. Guess I'll have to spell it out for him." Then he begins to speak in what sounds like an exaggerated slow style. "Now, Gus, you want to keep this diner going, and you want your staff to stay healthy, don't you?"

"What are you talking about?" Gus responds.

"Pay us fifteen percent of your take each week, and you'll be fine."

Gus's face turns red. "You're crazy if you think I'll pay you one cent. You can't just come in here and threaten us. Leave now or I'll call the police."

I pick up the phone and get ready to dial.

All four guys stand. "Aw, Gus, that wouldn't be smart. The cops won't save you, the diner, or your girls. We'll be back next Friday to collect and every Friday after that. Don't try to be a hero. We'll be watching." The gang swaggers out.

I join Gus at the rear table. "I notice they didn't pay their bill. Course that's small stuff compared to what they threatened. Should I call 9-1-1?"

Gus is standing where they left him staring at the ground. "They seemed confident the police won't help us. Something's not right. I want to talk to the other shop owners on this block to see if they know anything. Then I'll call the cops. Where did these guys come from, Suzanne?"

"I don't know. Never saw them anywhere else but here. They've only been coming in for a week. Should I tell Cheryl?"

"Nah, don't. Let's keep it between us for now. I hate they're threatening you. I'll finish up. Why don't you ladies go home. See you tomorrow."

"I'm almost afraid to leave you alone," I say.

"It sounds like nothing will happen until next Friday, so don't worry," Gus says as he returns to the kitchen.

I go up front and tell Cheryl we're free to take off. I look around our little place before I leave. The diner has ten booths down the one side and a long counter opposite the booths with seating for eight. The counter is made of Formica and is an off-white color. While it's in good condition, you can see the worn spots after decades of use. The entrance to the kitchen is at the far end of the bar. Gus's parents bought the place in 1945, and the building dates back to 1918. Even though it's old, it's comfortable. We keep it sparkling clean, and the dark red vinyl seating is in great shape.

This place has been my second home since high school when I started here. I can't stand the thought of those creeps threatening it. I close and lock the door and head for home.

Chapter 2

I arrive back at the diner the next day at 5 a.m. We begin prepping for our morning crowd. We open at six. Cheryl sticks her head in the kitchen. "First customer is at the bar, Suzanne."

"Okay, I'm coming." I get a glass of water and grab a menu for our early riser. "Good morning, and..." I'm startled because I'm looking at one of the guys who was with Scar Face yesterday.

"Hi, Suzanne. How are you?"

I didn't expect this. I take a deep breath and smooth my hair back."I thought no one would be coming back until Friday, and how do you know my name?"

"Don't worry. I'm just here for breakfast. I heard someone say your name. I'm Rob."

I pause. Maybe I'm overreacting. Best to be cool. "What can I get you? Would you like coffee?"

"Yes to coffee, and I'd like bacon, scrambled eggs, hash browns, and two pieces of toast."

"White or wheat?"

"Wheat." He smiles at me, and I notice his dimples, definitely better looking than Scar Face.

I pour his coffee and pass the order to Gus as I go back to the kitchen. "I can't believe one of those goons from yesterday came back already."

"Scar Face? Oh wow, now you have me calling him that." Gus shakes his head.

"Says his name is Rob. He seems a little nicer than Scar Far, and he's a lot better looking."

"They said next Friday. Want me to get rid of him?"

"Nah, I can handle him."

When I bring out his order, Cheryl is talking to him every chance she gets. I'm relieved to see it all looks harmless. She's cute, has light brown hair and a friendly personality. All our customers like her. I slip the plate of food and his check in front of him, refill his coffee, and make my exit.

By 8:30 the morning rush is over. We work at cleaning up and starting preparations for lunch. I go out to clean up the coffee urns. Romeo Rob, as I have nicknamed him due to his attractiveness, is still at the counter.

"Suzanne, come here."

"What?" I feel irritated with the tone of his voice.

"Quit sending your co-worker."

"I didn't send her. She's friendly. Our customers like her."

"Well, I want to talk to you. Take a break and meet me out back."

"We can talk here," I reply, fearing his intentions.

"I don't want to risk being overheard by your co-workers. Just meet me out back." He looks around as though checking for anyone who might be listening.

I shake my head. "I'm not going outside. Keep your voice down. Gus and Cheryl are too busy anyway. What do you want to tell me?" I ask.

Rob says, "Take Satchi seriously. He's dangerous."

"Yeah, I got that."

"I'm just trying to be sure you understand."

"What part of 'do as I say or else' do you think I don't get?"

"Just be careful, and tell Gus to do the same."

"This is what you wanted to say? Who are you, their PR guy? Or, are you trying to lull me into the delusion you want to help us?"

"Everything is not what it seems. Yes, I want you to trust me and cooperate for your own safety."

"I've no idea what you mean by 'everything is not what it seems'. You haven't told me anything. And, 'trust you'? That's a joke."

"You have no idea how violent Satchi can be. I know you don't know me or any of us. I guess I need Gus and you to realize how dangerous this situation is."

"I think I get it, but I don't understand why you guys are picking on us."

"I've said enough. Whatever you do, don't tell anyone we talked." Romeo turns, tosses money on his check, and leaves.

What the...what was that all about? What a con man. He wants to make me go along like I'm a partner with him. Boy, these guys are more devious than I thought.

***

After we finish for the day, Gus asks me to stay. Cheryl leaves, and Gus pours us a soda and motions me to sit down at the back table across from him. He tells me the other two shop owners--Alan, who owns the bookstore on the corner, and Joe, who owns the hardware shop next door--were also threatened. However, none of the owners across the street were bothered.

"What about the lady who owns the gift shop on our other side?" I ask.

"She's gone. There's a sign in her window saying she's on vacation. She usually doesn't stay away more than two weeks."

"What did Alan and Joe say?"

"They're outraged like me. None of us can afford to stay open if we're forced to pay. We want to go to the police, but Scar Face's warning is scaring all of us" Gus takes a sip of his drink. "He might be bluffing, but he seemed so sure the police wouldn't help us. It's hard to know what to do. If only the diner had been threatened, I would take the chance. But I can't stand the idea of either you or Cheryl getting hurt on my account."

"That Romeo Rob guy warned me to take Satchi, apparently that's Scar Face's real name, seriously."

Gus frowns. "When did you talk to him?"

"Remember, he came in early today?"

"Oh yeah, I forgot. Seems strange he warned you again."

"I thought so, too."

"Maybe he's our watcher, and the other two are watching Alan and Joe."

"Makes as much sense as anything. We need to do something about this."

Gus asks, "Like what?"

I shrug. "I don't know."

"Yeah, me either. Well, I better get the deposit in." Gus gets up and squeezes my shoulder as he passes to go back to the kitchen.

I finish up and head for home where I find Romeo Rob on my porch. "What the hell are you doing here?" I ask stopping on the front walk.

"Suzanne, I didn't like it when Satchi threatened you yesterday."

"Yeah, it didn't make my day either."

"You've got to take him seriously."

"You're like a broken record. I heard you the first time. Now get out of here."

"Let me in so we can talk. I'd like to get to know you." He smiles like he's an old friend.

"Hell, no. Go away." *What's he up to?*

Romeo Rob looks at me for a minute, then he nods and says, "Okay, you're right. I'll go, but if you need anything, call me." He shoves a card into my hand. "Leave a message to call. Don't say your name or number. Be careful, Suzanne." Then he's gone.

I go in and lock the door. *It's so weird Rob warning me again. What's going on here?*

***

Friday arrives. The intimidating four stay until our last customer has left. Then Satchi yells for Gus. I wait nervously in the kitchen until they leave.

I go out and join Gus. "You okay, Gus? How much did they make you pay?"

"Let's just say they won't have to protect this joint for long if I have to keep paying them. Maybe I should retire."

"I wish the whole group would drop dead."

"Yeah, the way I'm feeling, I would like to shake Satchi within an inch of his life." Gus squeezes a bottle of ketchup like it's Satchi's neck.

"Me too. I can't believe the police are in on it. I wish there was some way we could find out without Satchi hearing about it."

"That could be risky." Gus cautions.

I shake my head feeling frustrated. "This sucks."

"Promise me you won't do anything without checking with me first."

As I walk home, I give myself a pep talk. *This is a small town, and all 9,800 residents can't be involved in a conspiracy. I need to find some answers fast.*

Chapter 3

The following week is quiet. Satchi and gang don't come in until Friday. Satchi and two others march in. The one guy is tall and skinny. He wears a black baseball cap with no logo. The other one is medium height and looks like a fighter. Romeo Rob is not with them. At 2 p.m. Satchi yells for Gus. I wait in the kitchen in my usual spot by the food window. When they're gone, I go out.

"There were only three of them today. The guy you call Romeo wasn't with them," says Gus.

"Yeah, I noticed. Are you okay?"

"I'm too old for this, and retirement is looking better and better."

"Is that a possibility?" *Maybe that's a solution.*

"Money will be tight, but I think I've a plan that'll work. I didn't mention it before, but a developer contacted me wanting to buy this building."

"Really? That's good, isn't it? It sounds like a way out."

"Might be, but I turned him down. I wasn't interested in selling at the time. But now, everything has changed. I still have his card." Gus reaches for his wallet and begins going through it. Finally, he pulls out what looks like a business card.

"Great! Give him a call," I encourage looking up from a counter I'm wiping.

He asks, "What about you?"

"What about me?"

"We always thought you'd take over once I retired. Remember? We've talked about it."

I shrug. "Yeah, I remember, but that was before the gang arrived." Another idea hits me, "Say, you don't think this developer and the extortion stuff is connected?"

"Never occurred to me. But, the timing does look suspicious. If he's behind those crooks, he knows we can't win."

"I wonder how we can find out."

"Remember your promise not to play detective. You could get hurt."

I pat his hand. "Don't worry about me. I wouldn't know where to start. See you tomorrow." However, I do have an idea. I didn't tell Gus because I knew he wouldn't like it. I'm going to call Rob. He wants to talk, so why not give him a chance."

When I get home, I call the number he left and ask him to call me back. I fix a sandwich and wait for his return call.

"You call that a supper?"

I jump out of my chair knocking it over in my haste. "How did you get in?"

"I came as soon as I got your call. What's up?" Rob picks up my chair.

"I didn't say come over. You didn't answer my question. How did you get in?"

"You need a better lock. A sneeze could break the old one you have. Get a dead bolt and a new front door lock, and don't hide your spare key in such an obvious place."

"Thanks for the security check. Now, give me my key."

"You called me, Suzanne. What do you want?"

For a second, I'm distracted by his rugged good looks. "Who are you guys working for?"

"Ourselves, as far as I know," he says as he sits down.

"Where were you today?" I sit in my original chair. I push the sandwich aside as I've lost my appetite.

Rob frowns. "Did something happen?"

He almost looks worried. "No, but Gus and the other shop owners can't take much more."

"I know," he says as he puts his hand over mine .

I jerk away from his touch. "Where're you guys from?"

"Here and there. I was training a couple more guys to join us today."

"Great." *More thugs to harass us.*

"So, anything else?"

I decide to be blunt. "Are you working for the developer who wants to buy up this block of businesses?" As soon as it's out of my mouth, I fear I've said too much.

"I don't know. Only Satchi knows, and he keeps the details to himself. Please don't take this any further. You don't know Satchi like I do. If he thinks you're snooping or crossing him in any way, you're dead."

"You're scaring me."

"I'm trying to protect you."

"Why?"

He pauses. "It's complicated. Please be careful. And remember, no one can know we talked." Then he tosses me the key, turns, and exits as suddenly as he arrived.

What a confusing guy. I'm tempted to believe him, but I need to remember it's all an act.

***

Before going to work the next day, I do an internet search for information on development plans in Shipley. All I find is mention of the possibility of building exit ramps from I-75 to our town. No help there.

Once the lunch hour is done, I tell Gus what I found in my limited search. "Maybe the developer and this interstate thing are connected," I say as I put away dishes.

"It kind of makes sense, and I think it definitely makes sense for me to sell now. If the exits happen, this developer may go closer to the action to build a bigger restaurant or a fast food place."

"Do you really want to sell, Gus?"

He pauses, then says, "I didn't think I'd be doing it this soon or to anyone but you. But, I need to get something out of this place before I go bankrupt. I need money to survive. I can't let sentimentality distract me."

I see Gus's point, but it seems so unfair he's being forced into this action. Maybe I'm seeing it wrong. If I'm honest, all I can think about is what will I do if Gus's Place closes? I've been here for nine years. There are no other small restaurants in downtown Shipley, which is why this diner has done so well. Gus has taught me so much about running the place. I love it, and I love Gus. He's like a second father to me. I need to focus on helping him. I'm young. I'll have plenty of time to worry about my career later. So what's next? I need information.

***

The whole sordid routine plays out the following Friday. On Saturday when I show up at 5 a.m., I see fire trucks and a police cruiser parked in front of the bookstore. It appears the bookstore has been destroyed. I rush into the diner to find Gus. "What happened?"

"They burned down Alan's store, and he's in the hospital. He was severely beaten."

"How awful. Was it Satchi and gang?"

"I can't prove it, but that's my guess."

"The police are there. Now we can find out if they're involved."

"I don't think so. It gets worse. Alan said he couldn't pay any more extortion, so he went to the police Friday morning. And look where it got him. We've got to get out of here before we lose everything." Gus sighs as he grabs a skillet. "But, in the meantime, we still have a business to run."

I begin helping Gus in the kitchen. Meanwhile Cheryl is busy with all the prep work before we open.

As soon as the diner opens, the gang marches in. There are six of them now. They go to the back tables. Cheryl comes back to the kitchen. "They're insisting you wait on them, Suzanne."

"I don't like this one bit," says Gus.

"Me neither, but I'll be careful." I put on a poker face. I know Gus will be watching through the food opening.

"What can I get you guys for breakfast? Your water and coffee are coming." Cheryl brings them right on cue. I take the six orders and turn to leave.

"Hold on," Satchi says as he grabs my wrist. I instinctively jerk away, which seems to irritate him. I could swear he hissed.

"What?" I say rubbing my arm.

"You need to learn some manners. Awful things happen to people who aren't nice to us." The group snickers.

"Then don't grab me."

"You've got a real smart mouth." Satchi starts to rise.

"Just saying." I could feel sweat forming on my upper lip.

The guy, who looks like a professional fighter, puts his hand on Satchi's arm, and Satchi resumes sitting. "Whatever. Get our food, bitch."

I go back to the kitchen cussing under my breath. I hand the orders to Gus. We work in silence. We exchange a glance as I pick up the food and go back out. There are no more confrontations. The gang leaves after they eat, throwing their money on the table. I feel like screaming from the tension, but manage to keep it tucked inside as I work.

***

Once we finish for the day and Cheryl leaves, Gus and I have a chance to talk.

"Boy, talk about scary. When Satchi grabbed you, I almost lost it. Are you okay, Suzanne? He's such a jerk."

"Yeah, he is."

"After what happened to Alan, I'm worried about you living alone in that big old house."

"Please don't spook me. I'm wound up tight as it is."

"The police asked if I'd seen anyone at Alan's store last night." Gus lives in an apartment above the diner.

"Did you?"

"I saw someone running from the store, but I couldn't make out who it was. I called 9-1-1."

There doesn't seem to be anything else to say. After I leave the diner for the day, I go to the library in town. I figure it might be nicer than going straight home, as I don't know who might be waiting for me. I ask to see the newspapers dating back two years. I still can't understand why our block of businesses is so interesting to this developer. Is he going to build residential or commercial units? But why this particular block? And why now?

Even though the issues are all on-line, it still takes time to read through them. I finally get tired, call it a day, and decide to return tomorrow on my day off.

Chapter 4

I'm heading up to bed when Rob calls.

"What do you want?"

"Did you get new locks?"

"You called to check on my locks?"

"Yeah, that and what took you so long to get home?"

"Are you spying on me?"

"No, I'm just interested."

"I was looking through old news articles, if you must know."

He responds with what sounds like genuine interest. "What were you looking for?"

"Nothing special, I was checking out our competitors."

"Try again."

"It's really none of your business what I do, but I'm trying to figure out why a developer wants our block of businesses. It's not making any sense to me."

"It's for some kind of housing is how I heard it."

"For whom? We're just a small town."

"What are you, some kind of super snoop? Let it go. Knowing too much could get you hurt or killed."

"Why did Satchi threaten me?"

"I don't know. He likes intimidating people. Satchi is unpredictable and violent. Don't push him."

"I'm scared of him. Feel better? I hate what you guys are doing to Gus and the other shop owners. You're driving them out of business. You're ruining everything. I hate all of you." I sink down on the bed.

I hear him sigh, "I know it's awful, but you need to cooperate to be safe."

"Then there's nothing left to say."

Rob is silent for a few seconds. Then he says, "I don't want anyone to get hurt." Then he hangs up.

***

Morning comes after a restless night. I shower and resume my research. I have to use my own computer since the library is closed on Sundays. I read for a couple more hours, but nothing is jumping out at me. Why take the chance of building when nothing has been decided? Does the developer know something the rest of Shipley doesn't?

I decide to take a walk to break the monotony of this computer work. As I near the diner, I see a familiar woman looking into the window of the diner. She's my age or a little older and is dressed casually in a blouse and slacks.

"Can I help you? Gus's Place is closed on Sundays," I say as I approach her.

The woman turns and smiles. "Hi! I was hoping to find someone in. I'm Jessica Keyes. I'm a reporter for the Shipley News.

I shake her offered hand and respond, "Nice to meet you. I'm Suzanne Moore. I work here, and I think I've seen you in our place."

"I love your restaurant. I was hoping to talk with someone about the bookstore and its owner."

"I don't know too much about it, except Alan is still in the hospital."

"Yes, I know. Well, I guess I'll let you go."

"Before you go, maybe you could help me with something. I'm trying to figure out why a developer is so interested in buying this block of stores. Do you have any ideas?" *Am I saying too much? Should I tell her about the extortion?*

"What developer?"

"I don't know his name, but I know he's approached the bookstore, the hardware store, and Gus's Place."

"The town council is working to get access from I-75 to this town. They're hoping to attract some large companies to relocate here in an effort to build up the local economy."

"What would that have to do with our block of businesses?" I ask.

"Maybe the developer is looking to build some upscale living quarters, like condos, for people employed by those large companies."

"When will the accesses be built?"

Jessica shakes her head. "No decision has been made. The council's been lobbying for the access for about two years."

"See that's what doesn't make sense. There are no plans to even start the accesses. So why the rush to buy up these properties?"

Jessica takes out a notebook and pen. "Why do you think he's in a hurry? Maybe he has another project in mind. Do you think there's any connection to the fire in the bookstore?"

"I don't know. All I know for certain is he's approached all three shops. Good questions, though. No wonder you're a reporter." I look at my watch, "Oh gosh, it's getting late. I've got to go. Nice meeting you, Jessica." *I need to leave before I blab some more. I'm feeling paranoid.*

"Nice meeting you, Suzanne. If I can be of assistance, please call me. Here's my card. Feel free to call my cell anytime."

"Thanks! Bye." I head down the street and unexpectedly meet Rob.

"What're you up to, Suzanne?"

"Taking a walk to get some fresh air."

"Who was the lady you were talking with? I've seen her before, but I can't remember where."

"She works for the newspaper. I forget her name. I've got to go."

"Be careful," he says and walks away.

I walk home quickly, pour a glass of water, and settle on my couch to mull things over. *Could the developer know something our officials don't? I need to get his name from Gus. Does he have a connection with any of the large companies wanting to come here? Does he know Satchi? Was running into Rob just a coincidence? I hope I can trust Jessica, because she would know how to get the details we seem to need.*

***

The next day I tell Gus about my discoveries related to the interstate access in bits and pieces, and I ask him about the developer.

"His name is Jacob Reis. He's with Adams, Reis, Xavier, and Associates."

I frown as I try to connect that information. Finally I say, "Never heard of them. Where's their office?"

"I think they're based in Columbus," Gus responds.

"The capital?"

"Yeah."

"The decision about those accesses will be made in Columbus. Quite a coincidence the company is there, too."

Gus frowns. "What coincidence? You're not making any sense. There are hundreds of businesses there."

"I guess I am talking crazy. I want to understand what's going on, and I want to help you, Gus."

"I appreciate your efforts, but I'm scared for you to be digging into who knows what. You don't know who you can trust."

"True." *It's official, we're both paranoid.*

As I walk home, I can't get over how deceptively calm everything seems. The streets are quiet, and I can hear the wind rustling through the leaves. Then, I think about Alan in the hospital, Gus and Joe being victimized, and now I'm constantly looking over my shoulder. Our little town is growing more sinister by the day.

22

Chapter 5

With no signs of Satchi and gang during the week, I still feel the need to get my locks changed and even look into an alarm system, which turns out to be too expensive for my budget.

On Thursday at the diner, Gus seems more agitated. I guess Fridays are becoming unbearable. "Gus, are you okay?"

"No, Joe told me this morning he's definitely done paying the gang money. He says he doesn't even have enough to pay his bills."

"That's scary, he knows what happened to Alan."

Gus rubs his hand over his head. "Yeah, he knows, but what can he do? If I could help, I would. I feel awful."

"I can imagine. Has Alan remembered any more about the night he was attacked?"

"The last thing Alan remembers is talking to some detective at the station that morning. He has no memory of what happened next."

"How awful."

"We all agree it's a disaster and we have to sell. I want to fight. Trouble is I don't know who I'm fighting. I can't take on a group of thugs by myself. And besides, I don't know who's behind all this. Somebody a lot smarter than Satchi has to be calling the shots."

"I can't imagine you selling this diner."

Gus spreads his arms as though exasperated. "Me neither, but I can't continue like this."

"Before you sell, is there time for more research? I know I'm asking a lot and it's not my money, but maybe we can find a way out of this mess. Can you hang in there a little longer?"

Gus grimaces. "Maybe two weeks, but no longer. I appreciate what you're trying to do, but please be careful. I couldn't handle it if something happens to you. I think I'll go visit Alan and try to talk to Joe again."

"You be careful, too." I hug him, and he leaves. I finish cleaning up and as I'm throwing away the last of the full trash bags into the dumpster behind the diner, I'm surrounded by Satchi and four of his pack. Rob is not with them. We stare at each other. My heart is hammering in my chest.

"Ah, she exits." Satchi traps me against the dumpster by placing his hands on either side of my head. He smells like cigarettes and alcohol. His goons are snickering and eyeing me like a piece of meat. I feel defenseless.

I remain silent. I couldn't speak if I tried.

"What? You not happy to see me? Maybe we should go back inside and talk this over." Satchi begins to pull me over to the door.

I finally find my voice. "I don't have a key," I lie as I desperately try to think of how to get away. I try to break free from his grip.

Satchi grabs me and says, "Not so fast." Then he slobbers on my face.

"Hey! Were you going to start without me?" Rob joins us. "I thought this one was my treat." His words sound casual, but his facial expression doesn't match.

"You weren't around and we didn't feel like waiting. This bitch needs to realize I'm in charge. Have a front row seat, maybe you'll learn something, too."

Satchi lets go of me when he turns to face Rob. Now Rob reaches around him and grabs me by my ponytail. He pulls me to him and kisses me roughly. I struggle, try to pull away, and begin to cry.

The guy with the baseball cap steps between Satchi and Rob. "Let's get out of here, Satchi, before someone sees us."

Satchi nods. "I guess she gets the picture. Don't think this is over, bitch, just because lover boy saved you. I'll be back."

I sink to the ground as soon as they're out of sight and begin to hyperventilate. A few minutes later, Gus rushes out the back door.

"Suzanne, what happened? Are you okay? I just got back and saw you out here. Should I call an ambulance?"

"No, I'm okay...just my pride got hurt. Satchi and his gang were here and wanted to scare me. They succeeded."

"Come on up to my place, until you calm down." Gus guides me up the backstairs to his apartment above the diner.

I sit at the table in his kitchen. He pours us both a beer, and we drink in silence, which is just what I need. After we finish, I feel calm enough to go home.

"Thanks, Gus. I'm feeling better. I better go now."

"I'll walk with you."

Once we arrive, Gus checks the back door and all the windows. He kisses me on the forehead and leaves. I turn off the lights and collapse on the couch. I've no energy to go upstairs.

A few minutes later Rob calls. I'm not surprised to hear from him.

In what sounds like a concerned tone, he says, "Suzanne, are you okay? I'm sorry I was so rough. I had to make Satchi buy it."

I say nothing in response.

"Say something!"

"Who are you? You act like we're friends."

"Suzanne--"

"Oh yeah, you can't tell me anything."

"I wish I could--"

"But it's not safe. I don't need your fake concern."

"It's not fake, I'm on your side."

"You have a funny way of showing it."

"I realize it looks confusing. You have to be careful about who you trust."

"I DON'T TRUST YOU!" I'm screaming, feel hysterical, and hang up.

I start to shake, cry some more, and finally fall asleep emotionally exhausted.

***

I startle awake. Where am I? Oh yeah, I spent the night on the couch. My neck is killing me, but the coffee smells great. Coffee?

I jump up and go to the kitchen. Coffee is brewing, and there are two jelly donuts on a plate with a napkin. I run around checking both doors and all the windows as well as every nook and cranny. No one is here. I decide to take a shower and clear my head before breakfast. I've just polished off the last donut when my phone rings. The caller number is listed as unknown."

I hesitate before answering. "Hello?"

"Feeling better? How was breakfast?" It's Rob.

"Fine." I feel as flat as I sound. "I'm fine and breakfast was fine. I thought you gave back my key."

"You're welcome." Rob hangs up.

This is crazy. He treats me like a piece of trash, then turns around and acts all caring and gentle. But, he did save me from Satchi. Who is the real Rob? I shake my head. I can't let the guy get under my skin.

I grab my laptop to see what I can learn about ARX and Associates. Turns out they're architects, attorneys, and real estate developers. Nothing startling there. And, unfortunately, the site doesn't tell me if they're shysters. All their testimonials are good, of course.

A reporter could dig into Jacob Reis and his dealings. I'm calling Jessica and telling her about the extortion. The police know, and might even be involved. Maybe Jessica can find the connection.

***

When I get home from work the next day, I call Jessica. It goes to voicemail. I leave my name and number. A half hour later Jessica calls back. We agree to meet tomorrow at the park. After I hang up, Rob calls.

"Why are you calling me?" I sound more whiney than assertive.

"I wanted to check on you."

"For Satchi?"

"I know you don't believe me, but I'm trying to protect you."

"From you and your buddies?"

I can picture Rob rubbing his hand over his curly hair as he considers his answer.

I don't like his silence. "If you're not going to say anything, I have to go."

"What are you doing today?"

"That's none of your business. You really don't get boundaries do you?"

"I'm not the enemy here."

"You're kidding right? You, Satchi, and your gang are terrorizing us."

"Don't list me with those guys."

"What do you mean? You're always with them. Why would you deny it?"

"A shorter prison sentence."

"You're hilarious, but I'm not buying it. Is something else going on here?"

Rob hesitates, then repeats, "Are you meeting someone?"

"My boyfriend."

"Funny, I've never seen one around."

"Okay, okay, I'm meeting a girlfriend."

"You're impossible. I tried. Be careful and remember Satchi has you in his crosshairs."

"Like I could forget."

He hangs up, and I realize this conversation was almost enjoyable.

Chapter 6

Jessica and I meet in the park the next day as planned. It's a beautiful fall day--sunny, no wind, and a mild temperature. The grounds are not crowded. I keep glancing around to see if Rob, or any of the gang, is spying on us.

Jessica settles next to me on the bench. "So, Suzanne, what's on your mind?'

"I want to know why Jacob Reis is interested in buying our block of businesses."

"You mentioned the purchase before. I don't understand your concern. Developers like to get in during times of expansions. Why are you so bothered by it? Why not ask him directly what his plans are for these properties?"

"Wait, there's more. Once Gus and the other shop owners turned down his offer to buy, a group of tough-looking guys started extorting money from all three owners."

"That's awful. What did the police say?"

"Alan, who owns the bookstore, reported all this to the police. The same day his store was burned down, and he was severely beaten. He's been in the hospital for two weeks, and he has no memory of what happened."

Jessica is taking notes. "Do you think there's a connection between the developer, this gang, and the police?"

"Maybe, but how do we find out for sure? These jerks are dangerous. They pushed me around one night after work. I don't know what's going on or why. We keep getting warned not to go for help or snoop around."

After I finish talking, Jessica is quiet. She seems to be lost in thought. I look around again to be sure we're still alone.

Finally Jessica says, "You must feel like you're in a nightmare."

"We do."

"I want to help. I can't stand the idea this is happening in our town."

A sense of relief washes over me. "We sure need your help. Thank you!"

"Don't thank me yet. I'm not a detective, but I have resources. I need to do research on the developer and his company. Do you know the names of these gang members? I didn't know Shipley had any gangs."

"There are six of them, but I only know two names--Satchi, the leader, and another one is Rob."

"Hmmm...can't do anything with that. I'll see what I can find out and will call when I get something. If anything else happens, call me right away."

"Thanks, Jessica. You've no idea what this means to us. Please be careful. They're violent."

"I hear you. I'll be in touch. Bye." Jessica hurries off.

I head back home. Now I wait and hope I've done the right thing.

***

The next week is a repeat of the previous ones. Gus seems so discouraged and hopeless. He asks daily if there are any messages from Jessica. I hate my negative answers. We're all tense. Even Cheryl has picked up our moods. She has asked Gus and me what's wrong, but neither of us confide in her. So far no one has bothered her.

When I arrive on Saturday morning, Gus seems distraught.

"What's wrong?" I ask.

"Last night Joe was beaten, and there was a fire in his storage room. Luckily the fire department got there before it spread to the store's interior. It's mostly smoke damage."

"Oh my God, is Joe okay?"

"No, he's in critical condition."

"Was it Satchi?" I ask, even though I know the answer.

"No witnesses again. I heard a noise around two a.m. I thought I saw someone running away. It looked a lot like the guy you call Romeo. But, I can't be sure. I called for help and went down right away and found Joe lying in the alley by his backdoor. He was unconscious and bleeding profusely. It was awful. He was beaten savagely. When the medics arrived, they rushed him to the hospital.

"Joe must have refused to pay those guys, even though I begged him not to do it. I failed him." Gus sinks onto a stool and covers his face with his hands.

I put my hands on his shoulders. "This is not your fault. Didn't you tell me, before this mess all started, Joe was having financial problems with the hardware store? Why didn't he sell when the developer first approached him?"

"Yeah, I thought the same thing." Gus looks up. "Joe is a proud, stubborn man. I guess he wanted it to be his idea to sell." Gus shakes his head. "Everything keeps getting worse. We're being cornered with no way out."

***

When I get home, I call Jessica and leave a voicemail.

She calls back immediately. "Hi, Suzanne. I heard about the hardware store fire. How's Joe?"

"He's still in I.C.U. His shop wasn't destroyed, but he did get a lot of smoke and water damage in the storeroom. Have you found out anything?"

"Nothing helpful. So far the path leads back to the firm in Columbus. I know a lobbyist there I would like to question to see if he knows anything about Reis and these interstate accesses."

"Anything I can do to move this along?"

"Not really. I hear your frustration, but it takes time to find this type of information. Keep in touch. Along with my other work, I'm pursuing this every spare moment."

"Okay. Thanks. Bye." I hang up and feel swamped by my concerns. Nothing makes any sense. Gus saw Rob running away from the hardware store. I know he's one of the gang, but I was starting to think he was different.

***

I hadn't been asleep more than two hours, when I awaken to a noise coming from the back door. I grab my large, heavy flashlight from the dresser and creep down the stairs to the door. I peek out and see Rob leaning against the doorframe. He looks like he might fall at any time. I flip on the porch light.

33

Rob looks up at me. "Turn off the light."

I turn off the light and gasp, "What happened to you?"

Rob is a bloody mess. He groans, "Please help me. I don't have anywhere else to go."

"Who did this to you? One of your charming friends?"

"We had a disagreement. Can we talk about it later?"

"Sure," I say as I help him enter and take a seat at the kitchen table. I begin to assess his injuries. "I'll get the first aid kit."

Rob nods, and even this small gesture seems to cause him pain.

I gather wash cloths, towels, a variety of bandages, and some ointment. My mom, a nurse, liked to keep the first aid supplies well stocked. Somehow I know this isn't the type of emergency she envisioned.

I help Rob remove his shirt so I can wash away the blood. "You might be bleeding internally. I suspect you have at least one cracked rib. Are you having trouble breathing?"

"It's painful, but I think my lungs are okay. You're probably right about the rib, but I can't go to the hospital. They'll be looking for me."

"They? You mean Satchi?"

"Yeah, he's pissed at me right now. He's probably worried I'll snitch. I've got to lay low. Give him a chance to sober up."

As he talks, I'm becoming afraid. "Any chance the gang followed you here?"

"No, I was careful. I'm sure no one saw me come in."

Rob has many injuries to his face, chest, arms, and his knuckles. He put up a fight. I bandage as many of the deeper cuts as possible. Working together we get a large Ace wrap around his chest to help with the rib pain.

"Here, Rob, take these aspirin. Why don't you try to get some sleep. You can stay in the guest room."

He takes the tablets from my hand, drinks some water, stumbles up the stairs to the bedroom, and eases himself onto the bed. I turn off the light and go downstairs. I settle on the couch after checking to be sure the doors are securely locked.

Wow, now they're turning on one another. I wonder what the fight was about.

Suddenly, the phone rings.

I answer with much apprehension. "H-hello?"

I resume breathing when I recognize Gus's voice. "Suzanne? I keep thinking about what you went through today and couldn't sleep. Thought I would call and see how you're doing." There's a pause. "I'm so stupid. I just looked at the time. I hope I didn't wake you."

"No, you didn't. In fact, I just got up to take some aspirin."

"If you're okay, I guess I'll let you get back to bed. Goodnight."

"Goodnight and thanks for checking on me." I hang up. *Why didn't I tell Gus about Rob?*

***

I sleep a few more hours. When I wake up, I listen for any noises. I creep up the stairs. Rob is still in bed and appears to be asleep. I dress and go back downstairs. Needing to keep busy, I decide to focus my energy on fixing a big breakfast.

A short time later there's coffee brewing, fresh squeezed juice, bacon, and the eggs are almost done.

"Smells good in here!" Rob hobbles into the kitchen.

I hurt watching his labored moves. "Almost done. Want some coffee?"

"Love some," he says as he eases himself onto the chair.

"How are you feeling?"

"Better, thanks to you. In a couple days I'll be fine."

After we've been eating for a few minutes, I decide to push for details. "Why did Satchi turn on you?"

"It's complicated."

"Will we ever get past this cat and mouse game? I've had some college, I think I can follow."

"Satchi prefers only 'yes' men. I broke the rules when I interfered with him and you."

"What else was the disagreement about? He assaulted me a while back. Seems like a delayed reaction."

"Better I don't say. Satchi would be furious with both of us if he finds out we talked."

I shrug. "So would Gus, and you haven't told me anything. By the way, Gus saw you running from the hardware store the night Joe got attacked."

"What do you want me to say? You know I'm in this group."

My head knows, but my stupid heart wants a different answer from him. "Nothing makes sense. I get you're afraid to buck Satchi. But, you're hiding something. If you want me to trust you, how about you start trusting me."

Rob avoids looking at me directly. Finally he leans forward and says, "I've actually known you for a long time."

"What? How? I don't remember your coming to Gus's Place."

"No, not there. This is going to sound crazy." Rob takes a deep breath, and then he continues. "When you were fifteen, your parents were killed in a car accident caused by a drunk driver."

I gasp, "How do you know about my family?"

"The drunk driver was nineteen. He was my brother, Tom."

"Go on." I did not see this connection coming and don't know how to react.

"As you know, Tom was also killed in the wreck. My parents were heartbroken, not only because they had lost a son. They were horrified about your family being so cruelly torn apart. My dad never recovered. Six months after the accident, he died of a heart attack. Then mom and I were alone.

"Mom was concerned, almost to the point of obsession, with your welfare. She was relieved when your grandmother moved in with you. Over the years she watched from a distance when you graduated from high school, started college, and worked at Gus's Place. She worried when your grandmother died, but you were twenty-one by then. Before she died two years ago, she made me promise I'd look in on you occasionally to be sure everything was okay."

I'm shocked by his words and become lost in my memories of a very difficult time in my life.

"Say something, Suzanne." He covers my hand with his.

I gently pull away. "Wow, permission from your mom to stalk me. That's different. But, I was never your problem. Neither you nor your mother caused the accident. I guess I can understand your mom's concern. But, if the driver was her son and your brother, you both were grieving too. I know it turned my world upside down. But, I never needed you to watch over me. It's sort of kind, but is that what you think you're doing now?"

Rob almost looks sheepish. "When I joined that group, I never knew Satchi was going to target Gus's Place. Once I realized what was happening, I felt responsible for your safety. I went out of my mind when I realized the danger you would be in."

"What did your mom think about your hanging out with Satchi? She must have been so proud of your choice of friends."

Rob grimaces. "She never knew about Satchi. If I'd known you might be hurt, I would have done a lot of things differently. I'm afraid for you and the way you're going after answers."

"How else can I find out anything? The shop owners are losing their businesses, but we don't know why. The police aren't helping, and we don't know why. Someone has the answers. Why should I stop searching? Will you fill in the blanks? That's the kind of help I need."

Rob speaks in a soft voice, "It could get you killed."

"I can't just walk away from Gus. He's helped me in so many ways. If you're so worried about me, help me get the answers we need to stop Satchi and whoever is calling the shots. My money is on Reis."

"I don't know, Suzanne. It's not as easy as you're making it sound. If I leave the group now, I'll have a target on my back."

I wave my hand in his direction. "Looks like they've already turned on you."

"I'm guessing this was a warning not an expulsion." He seems to be lost in thought. Then he says, "But, maybe I can help. If I stay in the group, I might start hearing something useful."

"Are you being straight with me? "

"Yeah, I am. To make this work, we have to keep our friendship to ourselves."

"Friendship? Whatever. Okay, I won't tell anyone. Have you told me everything you know about this mess?"

"Yes."

"You better go. I've no desire for your gang to find us together."

Rob sits there for a while tapping his finger on the table.

"Do you have a safe place to go?" I ask.

"I'll go back to the motel. I might as well find out now if they're taking me back. I'll be in touch. Watch your back."

Chapter 7

The next day Gus asks me to stay after closing so we can talk. Once cleanup is done and Cheryl leaves, Gus pours us two cups of coffee. "Suzanne, I've decided to sell."

"I thought the attack on Joe might be your breaking point."

"You guessed it. I'm hoping, if I sell, the extortion and the threats will stop." Gus shakes his head. "*If* there's a connection between Reis and Satchi."

"I'm convinced there is."

"My biggest regret is I couldn't pass the diner on to you. It's been our dream for so long. It would've been like keeping it in the family."

I sigh. "I know. What're your plans after you sell?"

Gus shrugs. "Nothing definite yet, but I'm working on something. I'll have to find another apartment, and we both need to get on with our lives."

"I agree. I haven't given much thought to the future. I like restaurant work. Maybe I'll move to a new town, a larger one with more restaurants."

Gus looks sad. "I'd give anything if this wasn't happening."

I nod with understanding. "Me too. When are you planning on meeting with Reis?"

"I've set up a meeting for Thursday after we close."

"Can I be there?"

"Of course! I want you there."

***

Thursday arrives. Gus appears jittery all day, and I don't feel so calm either. At 4:30 Mr. Jacob Reis saunters in. He's a nice looking man of about forty. He's dressed in a business suit. Gus and I are standing by the end of the counter when he enters.

Reis smiles like he's greeting old buddies. "Hello, Gus! I'm so pleased you changed your mind about selling. Is this your daughter?"

"Mr. Reis, this is Suzanne Moore. She's like family, and we're partners here."

"Excellent. Then let's get down to business," says Reis as he sits at a nearby table. "I have the purchase agreement for you to sign. Miss Moore is not on the deed, but she can sign as a witness."

We join Reis at the table. Gus clears his throat and asks, "Your offer is $85,000?"

Reis gives Gus what looks like a pitying smile. "While $85,000 was my original offer, circumstances have changed, have they not?"

I want to slap his face. *Like you care.*

Gus looks like he's in shock. He says, "What do you mean?"

Reis shrugs, "Seems like crime has picked up in this area. A lot of violence tends to drive down property values."

Gus's eyes narrow. "I repeat, what do you mean?"

"I mean my offer is now $45,000."

"$45,000!" Gus yells as he jumps up. "You can't be serious. I can't let this place go for such a low price."

"Okay, okay, Mr. Breckman, take it easy. You can't blame me for trying." Reis waves his hand to take in the diner. "I'm a business man, and I like to negotiate the best price. But, I will agree to my original offer of $85,000."

I reach up and gently tug on Gus's arm to get him to sit. He plops down.

I say, "Mr. Reis, why don't you let Gus think over your offer for a few days."

Reis ignores me. "Mr. Breckman, you've had enough time. Either you're ready to sell or not. It's up to you."

Gus stares at his hands for a while.

"Mr. Breckman?" Reis prompts.

"Okay." Gus sounds like a deflating balloon.

"Gus? Are you sure?" I feel numb.

"What choice do I have?"

"Wonderful!" Reis points to lines on the sheets. "Just sign here and here. Miss Moore, please sign here."

As soon as Gus signs, he stomps out of the room.

I watch him leave, turn to Reis, and sign as the witness.

Reis hands me the carbon copies. "Tell Mr. Breckman we'll close in two weeks. The title company will notify you of the time and place." He puts the original contract into a case and leaves.

I'm in shock and can't seem to move. *The diner's gone. They won.*

***

Gus has little to say on Friday. I know we're both anxious to see if the extortion will stop. My heart sinks when I see the group come in and go to their regular table.

At 2 p.m. they call for Gus. "You know the drill, old man. Pay up."

Gus whispers, "No."

I hold my breath as Satchi is momentarily silenced. I look around for a weapon and grab an iron skillet.

Satchi jumps up, "What did you say?"

"The diner is closing. I have no money to give you. Your partner is getting this place, so no more 'protection' needed. Get the hell out of my diner."

Satchi gets close to Gus and hisses, "That's got nothing to do with us, fool. Either you pay or you're done and so is your bitch."

The group strut out.

"Gus! You took quite a chance." I rush out still clutching the skillet.

Gus slams his fist on the counter as he declares, "I'm done being a doormat. If they come after me, like they did Alan and Joe, I'll be ready to defend myself and my property."

"How can I help?"

"You can't. Leave town. You heard the monster. They want to hurt you."

"I'll go if you'll go with me."

Gus puts his hands on my shoulders. "This is my fight, not yours."

I shrug off his hands. "Oh no you don't. This is our fight."

"I can't do this if I have to worry about you." Gus has a forlorn look on his face.

"Guilt won't work. If we go down, we go down together."

Gus gives me a bear hug. "I guess we need a battle plan."

I nod in agreement. But no matter what I said, I'm terrified for both of us for what the night might bring.

As we prepare to close up, my phone vibrates showing a text message from Rob encouraging me to have Gus stay at my home where we'll be safe.

Rob's right about one thing, Gus and I are safer together. If Satchi follows his pattern, Gus's Place will be burned down tonight.

I go to the kitchen where I find Gus staring at the wall. "Gus, how about you stay at my place tonight?"

"I won't run like some spineless coward."

"Believe me, no one would accuse you of being chicken. Truth is, I'm afraid to be alone tonight."

"Which is why you need to leave town. You could stay with my sister in Indianapolis."

"Let's both go, Gus."

"No. I have to draw the line somewhere, and this diner is mine until closing."

Is he determined to die? "Okay, Gus, so be it. I stand with you. I'll stay here tonight."

Gus puts his hands on his hips in confrontation. "Absolutely not. Why are you so stubborn?"

"I'm stubborn? We're family. You said so yourself."

Gus relaxes his stance and chuckles. "You're crazy, but I love you. Okay, if it makes you feel better, I'll stay at your place for the time being. Let me pack a bag. Tomorrow we open as usual."

I give him a salute as he heads for his apartment. *Will there be a diner tomorrow?*

I call Jessica while I wait for Gus. "Hi, Jessica, have you found out anything?"

"Nothing concrete. Rumors are some palms in the legislature are getting greased, but I have no proof. It's tough identifying all the players. Once I narrow it down, I'll start the background checks."

"Start with Jacob Reis. He just got Gus to sell the diner. My money is on him as the kingpin, but I don't know why he's doing it."

"You guys need to get out of town before there's more violence."

"Yeah I agree, but Gus won't go. And I won't go without Gus. We're running out of time. Closing is in two weeks."

***

After we get to my place, we eat, and settle in for the night. Around midnight, Rob sends another text telling me we're safe. He says he and his friends will guard the house.

I text back, "Satchi?"

Rob writes, "NO. Friends from out of town. Satchi knows nothing. Does Gus know about us?"

I shake my head and then realize he can't see me. I send, "No."

***

Following our routine, Gus and I return to the diner the next morning. We unlock the front door and stop. The place has been trashed but not burned down. Stools are broken, booth seats are slashed, tables are horribly scratched, and behind the counter is a complete disaster. The coffee urns arc smashed as well as the beverage fountain. The countertop has been spray painted, "Fuck you". The walls are covered with paint splashes.

We make our way to the kitchen. The back door is wide open. The stove and dishwasher appear heavily damaged. The refrigerator and freezer doors have been left open. Food is thrown everywhere.

Gus and I look at each other. Then Gus says, "Wonder why they didn't burn it down? Took time to do this much damage, and--"

Gus is interrupted by screaming in the front room. We rush out of the kitchen to find Cheryl sobbing.

She looks at us and cries, "What happened?"

"We're in trouble," Gus responds, as he looks around forlornly.

"What kind of trouble?"

"That group of guys who've been coming in every Friday are extorting money from me. I refused to keep paying after I agreed to sell this place to a sleazebag developer."

"You're being extorted, and you sold this place? Did you know about any of this, Suzanne?"

I know she's not going to like my answer. "Yes."

"How long?" Cheryl snapped.

I hesitate before answering. "Since it started about four weeks ago."

"Well thanks a heap for letting me know. I care about this place, too."

Gus replies, "Of course you do, Cheryl. We wanted to spare you. We were worrying enough. No need to make you miserable too."

Cheryl still looks pissed. "Have you called the police?"

I pull out my phone. "Not yet, but I am now."

"Suzanne?" Gus turns to me.

"We've been quiet long enough. You said you wanted to draw your line here. Let's find out if the police are involved."

Gus nods slowly saying, "Okay."

While we wait, Gus calls his insurance agent. He has to leave a voicemail due to the early hour. We remain standing like statues in the same spots until the police arrive. We're introduced to a Detective Jones. He's as tall as Gus but a few years younger.

He begins to question us. "Do you have any idea who did this, Mr. Breckman?"

"Yeah, I suspect this no-good group of guys who've been extorting money from me for the last four or five weeks. Yesterday I refused to pay anymore. They said and I quote, 'You're done and so is your bitch'."

"Why didn't you report this sooner?"

I decide to join the conversation. "Joe Sachs and Alan Sutton did file reports with you. They were severely beaten, and their stores were set on fire. Where have you been? What have you done about it?" I'm feeling angry and overwhelmed.

"Miss Moore, this is the first I've heard anything about beatings or a gang behind it. It was my understanding the fires were accidents. I've been on vacation. So, catch me up. What are the names of the members of this gang? Where are they from?"

"Satchi is the leader, and one of the other guys is Rob. I don't know any other names."

"What about you, Mr. Breckman?"

"Same as Suzanne. It's not like we have a friendly relationship with any of them."

"Well, only first names isn't much help. We might get fingerprints here. If you'll come to the station, Mr. Breckman, you can look through our books or maybe talk with our sketch artist. Do you have any idea where they live?"

I say, "I thought I heard them say something about a motel."

Gus looks around forlornly at the mess. In an exasperated tone he says, "Sure, detective, I can go with you. Obviously we can't open for business. Suzanne, call someone to fix the back door. We'll have to inventory the damage, including all the spoiled food. Hopefully the equipment can be fixed. Once the insurance guy gets everything he needs, we can start cleaning up the mess before it starts to smell. You'll both be paid for today."

Cheryl and I agree to follow Gus's instructions. We wait for the police to take their pictures and finish collecting fingerprints. I call our handyman and explain the damage to the back door. He agrees to come in an hour. The insurance agent calls back and is due in an hour also.

After Gus leaves, Cheryl confronts me. "Why didn't you confide in me? Aren't we friends? Didn't I have a right to know?"

I squirm as I answer, "You're right. We shouldn't have kept you in the dark."

"I heard about Joe and Alan's injuries. Thank goodness neither of you have been attacked."

"That's not exactly true. About a week ago, those guys cornered me and scared the bejeebers out of me. Luckily I wasn't hurt."

Cheryl squeezes my hand. "Sounds awful."

"Yeah, it was. We all need to watch our backs."

"I don't get why the police haven't stopped them."

"Gus and I don't understand it either. We're suspicious of a connection between the police and whoever is behind all this."

Cheryl asks, "What kind of connection?"

"Before the gang came, a developer tried to buy all three places. All the owners refused to sell. Enter the gang. Satchi said the police wouldn't help, and they didn't help Alan or Joe."

"Wow, it does sound suspicious, but what's the point? Why does anyone want this block of buildings?"

"We don't know, but the rumor is the developer wants to build condos or some type of fancy living places. I asked a reporter to find out for us, but so far she's had no luck. I think I'll call her and tell her about this mess."

Jessica answers immediately. "What's up, Suzanne?"

"Gus's Place was vandalized last night. It's so bad, Gus may not be able to re-open before the sale closes."

"Are you there now?"

"Yes."

"I'm on my way with John, my photographer. Your best bet is to get as much exposure as possible."

"Makes sense to me. See you soon."

Ten minutes later Jessica and John arrive. Jessica interviews Cheryl and me while the photographer takes pictures of everything including us. Jessica decides to wait on Gus, who's still with the police.

The handyman and the insurance agent arrive and begin their work. As soon as they leave, I grab garbage bags, and Cheryl and I begin the massive food cleanup in the kitchen.

I hear the front door open, and then I hear Jessica introducing herself to Gus. She begins to interview him. Then the door opens again, and there is silence.

"My oh my, what a mess." I hear Satchi and am guessing his gang must have entered.

"Get out!" Gus shouts.

"Chill, old man. We're here to give you some sympathy. Who're your friends? Hey, dude, you better put down your camera before I smash it."

Jessica says, "I work for the newspaper. My photographer meant no harm. He won't take your picture if you don't want him to do so."

"Well, I don't. There's no story here."

"There's always a story," responds Jessica.

"What did I tell you, guys? Everyone around here has a smart mouth. Wouldn't you agree?"

I peek out to see Satchi's sneering cohorts form a half circle around Gus, Jessica, and John. I've heard enough and fear the worst, I call 9-1-1 and report the attack.

Then I walk out front. "You guys might want to leave since we're about to have company."

I could hear a siren approaching. Satchi motions for his guys to exit. Both Satchi and Rob look back at me.

Then Satchi says, "I won't forget this, bitch. You'll be sorry." He slams the door as he walks out.

Jessica says, "Whew, Satchi is a mean one." She puts her notebook and a small recorder in a pocket.

"So we noticed," says Gus wiping his brow.

"The one guy, not Satchi, kept looking at you, Suzanne. Do you know him?"

"Only from around here. He's a smartass and a flirt." *Another chance to tell about my relationship with Rob, and I don't.*

Jessica looks at me with raised eyebrows but says nothing. John and Jessica leave a short time later.

We continue cleaning the kitchen. Nothing can be saved. The back door is secured. Cheryl leaves after agreeing to come back if needed. Gus calls the insurance agent, who promises to process his report as soon as he's sure he has everything.

After a quiet evening at my place, we say goodnight. I know I feel emotionally drained, and it looks like Gus feels the same way. I wonder if Rob will call tonight.

Chapter 8

On Monday morning Gus and I go in to the diner to meet again with the insurance agent. I bring my laptop to show him the pictures Jessica sent me from Saturday. The agent arrives, looks over our photos, and takes more pictures. He asks me to send Jessica's pictures via his email and tells us he'll have the report within forty-eight hours. Gus explains he basically needs a new door, kitchen appliances, beverage machines, and money to restock enough food for a week. He says he's planning to close Gus's Place a week from this coming Saturday. He wants to reopen the place for the six days before closing. The agent discourages the idea of reopening and recommends using the money for a new venture, since it sounds like the diner might get torn down.

After the agent leaves, Gus says, "He's right. I don't know what I was thinking trying to get this place going again. I..."

His phone rings. "Hang on...Hi, Marty. What's up?" Gus listens for a few moments. "You're sure she's going to be okay?" He listens a while longer. I can tell by his expression something is wrong. "Sure, I can help. Let me make some arrangements here. I'll be there by tonight. Bye."

Gus hangs up and stares at his phone for a moment. I give him time to digest this latest problem.

"Suzanne, my sister in Indianapolis was in a bad car wreck. She's in the hospital in serious condition."

"I'm so sorry. Do they think she'll be okay?"

"They're saying it'll take time. There's an even bigger problem. Shirley, my sister, takes care of our invalid aunt. There's no one who can care for my aunt until my niece, who lives in Chicago, arrives. She should be there by next Saturday."

"Of course you need to go, Gus. There's nothing to do here before the sale."

"Maybe the insurance money will come this week. That'd speed things up with planning my future."

I reply, "Sure would."

"Suzanne, why don't you come with me?" Gus coaxes.

"I'd only be in the way. Besides, it'll be good for you to get completely away from here."

"What'll you do while I'm gone? Will you be safe?" Gus frowns and looks worried.

"I can keep an eye on this place. And yes, I'll be careful. I need to begin my job search. I've no idea where I want to go or what I want to do once your place closes."

"I know our recent troubles have gotten you down, but I'm sure there are many avenues for you to try."

"I know you're right. I've just never been completely on my own. It's something new to get used to. But, enough about me. What would you like me to do to help you get ready?"

"Just one thing before I go. I want those cuss words off the counter."

Gus has some paint remover, and we work on the countertop, removing the obnoxious words and polishing it as best we can.

Gus wipes his hands clean. "Not perfect by any means, but it makes me feel better."

I reply, "It looks better than I thought it would. I was beginning to think the stupid message would never be erased. I wish we could get rid of the gang the same way."

"Me, too. If you'll wait, I'll pack my bag. My bus leaves in an hour at 4:30."

The bus station is on my way home. We walk the two blocks in companionable silence. Truth be told, I'm not sold on staying here without him. I hug Gus and kiss his cheek before he boards the bus.

"Suzanne, please call me if anything looks even a little bit suspicious. Promise?"

"I promise. Bye for now. I hope your sister recovers quickly." I wave as the bus pulls away.

***

When I get home, I know I'm not alone. For one thing, there's a fire in the fireplace.

"Who's here?" I shout, although I have a good hunch.

Rob comes out of the kitchen. "It's only me, Suzanne. Are you hungry? I've a pizza and a cold beer waiting for you."

"What're you doing here?" I sit at the table and look around.

"It's okay, I'm alone. I want to spend some time with you, and I know Gus went to Indianapolis."

"How do you know about Gus? How're you getting in?"

"I overheard you talking at the diner. I'm sorry about his sister's accident."

"When were you in the diner? I never saw you."

"Guess I'm sneaky." Rob grins.

I lose my train of thought temporarily. "And what about the key?"

"I made a copy of your key. I planned to use it only in an emergency. Actually, you here alone might turn into one. I'm here to prevent that."

I shake my head in doubt. I didn't anticipate his company, but I'm glad I'm not alone. I grab a slice of pizza and am surprised by how hungry I am.

"Tell me more about yourself," Rob says as he grabs a slice.

"You first."

Rob shrugs. "Well, I'm not from around here. I grew up on a farm in Stockton. That's a rural area southwest of here. Now I live in Kingston. It's about an hour away. I had an older brother, Tom, but he died when he was nineteen. You know the story."

"Just you and Tom?" I ask.

"Yeah. Now I know some things about you, as I shared before. Tell me more."

"Not much to tell you don't already know. During high school I worked part-time for Gus. I used the insurance money from my parents and got an associate degree in restaurant management. After I completed my degree, I worked full-time at the diner. Gus taught me how to run the place and how to cook. Our plan was he'd retire whenever he wanted, and I'd take over the business."

"Sounds nice."

"It was until your bad-ass crew arrived."

We stare at each other for a moment.

Rob stands up. "I think we need another beer."

We take our drinks to the living room. I sit on the couch and Rob sits close to me. I don't object. In fact, I'm liking it. Settle down, I tell myself. He's part of a gang. No matter how nice he's behaving, he's up to something. I can't trust him no matter how much I want to.

I decide to try a change of subject. "I think it's time for you to tell me more about you. Why did you decide to join a gang?"

Rob is quiet for a moment. Then he says, "You deserve to know more, but you have to keep it confidential."

"I will." I sense his seriousness, and I want my promise to match his intensity.

"I'm a private investigator, and I'm working undercover. I was hired by a family, the Hoskins, to find the murderer of their son. The investigation brought me to Satchi, Todd, and Luke. I'm trying to get evidence on them. When we came to Shipley, everything got complicated." Rob takes out his wallet and shows me his license.

"Wow, I never guessed this twist. Is the story about your mother and brother true?"

"Yes."

"What made you become a P.I.?"

Rob gives me a sheepish smile. "I helped my mom find out about you, and my career started."

I return his smile. "When it's just the two of us, you never act like a gang member. But, I was finding it hard to trust you."

"And now?"

"I'm getting there. Trust isn't automatic."

"True."

I gaze at him for a minute, then I nod my head as I decide to try to believe he's telling me the truth.

Rob puts his finger under my chin and turns my face towards him. "Thank you. I won't let you down." Then he begins to kiss me. I return kiss for kiss. We're on the couch one minute, and then we're lying on the rug in front of the fire. We're caressing and kissing each other with a growing heat.

Rob pauses and looks at me as if asking permission and says, "Is this okay? Are we moving too fast?"

I pull his head back down and caress his head of curls I so like. *I'm enjoying this. But damn, he's right.* I pull away slightly and say, "You're right. We need to slow down."

Rob follows my lead and lies quietly. We don't let go of one another. Rob pulls an afghan off the couch and covers us. I fall into a deep, peaceful sleep.

Chapter 9

When I wake up the next morning, I'm alone on the rug. The fire is out, and Rob is gone. The house is silent. I go upstairs to shower. As I stand letting the water wash over me, I feel warm and content. I start to replay last night's conversation and the unexpected turn of events. Rob is a good guy. *Thank goodness.* I dress and go downstairs combing my damp hair.

"Good morning, sunshine!" Rob is busy putting out bagels, cream cheese, and marmalade. Coffee is brewing and glasses of orange juice are on the table.

"This is a surprise. I thought you left."

"I did go out to get some groceries," Rob replies.

I begin digging into this simple but satisfying breakfast, and he joins me. "Do you have any house repairs needing attention?"

"Are you staying?"

"Yes, while Gus is away. I don't want you to be alone here."

"Won't your gang miss you?"

"They think I'm out of town for a while."

"If I'm alone, do you think they'd try to hurt me." *Maybe I should have gone with Gus.* I feel fear growing.

"I'm not taking any chances. I'm also concerned about your reporter friend. I hope she prints her story soon. Once she does, Satchi will have less reason to hurt her. Can you give her a head's up?"

"Sure, but I imagine she's already figured that out. By the way, is your last name really King?"

Rob chuckles."It's my work name, my mom's maiden name. My legal name is Clinger. I don't want anyone to know it."

"Okay, I'll keep it to myself. But, what's the big mystery? Your gang knows, right?"

"No, we don't know each other's full names."

"How strange. How long have you been with them?" I ask.

"Two months. Satchi and the two original guys have been together for a while."

"None of you are from around here, right?"

"Those three are from Columbus, and I'm from Kingston, as I mentioned before."

"How did you get in with Satchi?"

"I got interested in him because of the murder investigation I was working on. I made sure our paths crossed."

"Do you have enough evidence to prosecute them?"

"A little more would work better. I haven't given up hope of nailing them."

While Rob is busy repairing the runner on the stairs and the leaky faucet in the bathroom, I call Jessica, but she doesn't answer. I leave a voicemail to call me.

There's no immediate return call. Although that's not unusual, I have an eerie feeling I can't shake.

Rob comes into the kitchen. "The stairs and the faucet are fixed. Do you have anything...what's wrong?"

"Jessica hasn't called back, and it's been an hour. She usually calls within fifteen minutes. I'm worried."

"Where does she live?"

"I don't know. Her last name is Keyes."

Rob takes out his phone and begins tapping in something. A short time later he gets a response. "She lives at 229 Olive St., apartment Four A."

"How did you find her address?"

"Trade secret." He winks at me. "I think I'll go by her place and check out if everything is okay."

I ask, "Wouldn't it make more sense if I go?"

"You're right. How about we both go, and I'll stay out of sight. It's safer if we're not seen together. "

I grab my jacket and head out. The streets are quiet as I walk to Jessica's place. I arrive at her apartment ten minutes later. Her car is in the parking lot adjacent to her building. I buzz her unit and wait for a response. There's none. I try once more with the same lack of answer. I go inside when I find the outside door is unlocked. I knock loudly on her door and call her name. No answer.

Rob joins me, he tries the door, and it opens. We enter and he motions for me to stay put as he does a quick walk around. The apartment is a shambles. Cushions are torn off the couch, desk drawers pulled out, and the contents dumped. Her purse has been emptied and the lining torn to shreds.

Rob returns and puts his arm around my shoulders. "Suzanne, Jessica is dead."

"What? How? What do we do now?" I can't seem to think straight.

Rob responds in a quiet, calm voice. "My guess is it happened during the night. She was shot in the head. No one else is here. I want you to call the police after I leave. Tell them you found her in bed. There's no pulse. Then go outside and wait for them to come. Before you call, we need to find her notes, if they're still here. Did she have a laptop yesterday? I didn't notice."

"No, she carried a recorder and a small notebook."

"Well, if Jessica used a laptop, there's no sign of it here."

Thinking about his remark, I have an idea. "Come to think of it, I saw her place both the recorder and the notebook in an inside pocket of her jacket after your gang left yesterday."

Rob gives me a pair of gloves. I now notice he's wearing a pair also. As we go into Jessica's bedroom, I stop at the sight of her in bed. An overwhelming feeling of guilt washes over me. *This is my fault. I got her into this mess.*

"Suzanne." Rob motions me to come over to the closet.

I begin looking for the jacket Jessica had on when we saw her at the diner. I spot it and locate the zippered pocket. The recorder and notebook are still there. Rob puts them in his pocket.

"Whoa, I want to see those."

"You will, back at your place."

"Are you taking them to Satchi?"

"No way. I want to keep these from him as much as you do."

Rob does a quick check of the mess around her desk but finds nothing.

He repeats his instructions, kisses me on the cheek, and leaves.

I make the call, go outside, and stuff the gloves deep in my pocket. While waiting, I relive the horrible moment when I saw Jessica in her bed. *I hope she didn't suffer. When will this end? How many more people will be hurt? Who's doing this and why?*

***

The police arrive and tell me to stay put. Detective Jones arrives, goes inside, and comes back outside to talk to me. "Do you have any idea who might have shot her, Miss Moore, or what they were looking for in there?"

"My guess is the gang we told you about is responsible. They threatened her yesterday at the diner." I go on to describe our encounter, "Detective, I'm worried about her photographer. He was at the diner with her."

"What's his name?"

"His first name is John, but I don't know his last name. I'm sure the newspaper office will tell you."

Detective Jones makes a few calls and then turns back to me. "What're you doing here?"

"When Jessica didn't return my call and wasn't in the office, I got concerned."

"How did you get in?"

"Both the outside door and her door were unlocked. I knew something was wrong. So I went in and found her."

"Do you know any other stories she was working on?"

"All I know is she was looking into ARX and Associates and a lobbyist who is working for them in Columbus. I think it had something to do with Shipley getting interstate access. Apparently a casino and some other big businesses are showing interest in this area if the access happens."

Detective Jones makes a few notes. "Thank you, Miss Moore. Please make yourself available if I have more questions. Would you like a ride home?"

"Thanks, I would."

"Are you working in the diner today?"

"No, Gus has decided not to reopen. He's in Indianapolis until Saturday helping a family member."

As I exit the car, he says, "Be careful, Miss Moore."

I nod and start up my walk. I keep fighting the urge to run. I've never been so scared.

***

Rob comes in shortly after me.

"Did the gang do this?"

"It looks suspicious, but Satchi is more violent and out of control. This looks more professional. The killer probably used a silencer. Let's take a look at her notes. Go ahead and start. I want to take a quick look around here to be sure we're alone."

64

I'm reading her notes when Rob comes back. He starts up the recorder. We hear Jessica's thoughts regarding the developer, ARX, and their possible ties to the State Department. Apparently she planned to go to Columbus this Thursday to interview the lobbyist, John Stacy. She makes a note to check out family ties. Then we hear the entire scene at the diner--the interviews with me, Gus, and then the gang. Satchi's voice is distinctive and menacing. The machine clicks off, and then comes on again. Jessica recorded, "There might be something going on between Suzanne and Rob, one of the gang members. I need to warn her to be careful as Satchi seemed to catch the look, too."

I look at Rob.

A frown creasing his forehead, he says, "I sure hope she's wrong about Satchi noticing anything between us."

"Me too. I've been trying to be careful."

Rob nods and then says, "Yeah well, we can be thankful the killer didn't find these materials. My guess is their next stop will be the newspaper."

"Do you still think she had a laptop?"

"I'd bet on it. If she did, most likely the killer has it."

Now what? Is there enough for the D.A.? Should I let Gus know what happened? Do I tell him about Rob? Too many questions.

I go back to reviewing Jessica's notes. I keep feeling like I'm missing something. *I wonder if the lobbyist knows Jessica won't be coming on Thursday. If he knows, does it mean he's connected to her killing and this whole evil mess?*

Rob leaves the room, and I take advantage of his absence to call Gus.

"How's your sister?"

"She's still in the hospital, but she's showing signs of recovering." Gus sounds tired.

I hate to add to his concerns, but here goes. "I have some bad news. Jessica, the reporter, was murdered last night. I don't know where the photographer might be. But if he doesn't know about Jessica, he needs to be warned. Her place was ransacked, but I found her notes and recorder."

"This is awful. Please, please come to Indianapolis. I'm afraid for you, especially if anyone finds out what you discovered."

"The police know about the murder. Detective Jones seems to be working with us. I plan on giving him these materials rather than keep them at my home."

"Good, the sooner you do the better. Please be careful. Satchi is treacherous."

"I'm being careful. I know this is going into deaf ears, but try not to worry. You have enough going on there to keep your blood pressure high."

"I'll be back just as soon as my niece gets here."

"Great. I'm looking forward to your return. Let me know if you hear from the insurance agent."

"Will do. Bye, Suzanne."

"So, you're planning on giving the notes and recorder to Detective Jones?" Rob must have come back into the room while I was on the phone.

"Yeah, I think it's the best move. I'm too nervous to keep them here."

Rob pauses as though he's considering the options. Then he says, "You'll have to explain how you found them and why you didn't give them to him immediately. You could be in serious trouble for tampering with evidence."

"I hope not, but no matter the consequences for me. The detective needs them. I assume you don't want me to mention you."

"Right."

I call the detective. He tells me he's on his way. I inform Rob.

"I'll go upstairs while you talk with him." He heads for the stairs.

Detective Jones arrives a few minutes later. I invite him into the living room. There're no signs of Rob or our night on the floor. Only one beer bottle remains on the table.

The detective appears to be struggling to control his temper. In an angry tone, he demands, "Miss Moore, why didn't you give me these items at the scene?"

"I know I should have. Blame it on paranoia. I wanted to see the contents before they disappeared. This is the last contact I'll ever have with Jessica. I already feel guilty for her death. I don't want to be the one who loses her notes."

"How are you responsible for her murder?"

"Jessica was trying to help Gus, me, and all the shop owners. She wanted to protect her town."

"How did you find the notes? Her apartment was torn apart."

"Yesterday I noticed Jessica placed both the recorder and the notebook in an inside pocket of her jacket and zipped it shut."

"Since you swiped them, I assume you read the notes and listened to the tape?"

"Yes."

The detective sighs. He seems exasperated as he says, "Well, what did you find out?"

"Jessica set up an interview with a lobbyist, John Stacy, for Thursday in Columbus. Also, she thought I have some kind of connection with one of the gang. I don't, and I told her the same before she left the diner yesterday." *I'm becoming an accomplished liar.*

"Is that everything? Miss Moore, do not withhold evidence ever again. I should charge you, but I won't. This is the only chance I will give you."

"I'm sorry, Detective. I won't do it again. Did you locate the photographer?"

"Not yet."

I nod and say, "I called Gus to let him know what happened."

"Good. I'll be in touch, Miss Moore. Please don't leave town without telling me.

After the detective leaves, Rob comes downstairs.

I ask, "What do we do now?"

"We need to lay low for your safety. Whoever we're dealing with means business."

"I gave the detective everything. Jessica possibly would have discovered the truth behind this mess, but I still know nothing."

"As long as they think you know something, you'll be in danger."

"Do we have enough to show the district attorney?"

"No. Hunches are worthless. The D.A. can't make a case out of thin air."

And here we are, back where we started.

***

Rob gets us two beers and sits next to me on the couch. We don't speak for a long while. I'm lost in my thoughts.

Rob says, "Do you mind if I order pizza again?"

"Okay."

"Would you like another beer?"

"Okay." I know I sound as down as I feel.

"Suzanne?"

I burst into tears. Rob wraps his arms around me while I sob into his chest. When I'm finally breathless and gulping for air, he gets me a box of tissues.

"I know, it's been a hard day."

"It's been awful," I gasp.

Rob nods. He calls in the pizza order and hands me twenty dollars. "It's better if I stay out of sight. Here's money for the pizza."

While Rob is out getting wood for a fire, the doorbell rings.

Clutching the twenty dollar bill, I go to the door. "Hi..." I stop. I'm face-to-face with Satchi.

"Well, Ice Queen, I know I'm irresistible, but you'll need more than twenty dollars to win my favors." He sneers and flicks my chin with an upward thrust of his right index finger.

"Unless you're delivering pizza, this isn't for you. What do you want?"

"I seem to have misplaced one of my guys. Have you seen Rob?"

"How would I know where he is? Good-bye."

"What's the hurry? Maybe we should get to know each other up close and personal. I'm more experienced at fucking than Rob."

I stand with my back against the door frame. I worry Rob will walk in on this scene.

"Shut the door. I'm not leaving."

"Either you do or I will. I'm not in the mood for company."

"Well, get in the mood, bitch. I have some questions you're going to answer one way or the other."

I try to get my purse off the hook by the door. Satchi grabs my arm and drags me from the wall into the living room.

"What do you want?"

"Many things, but I'll start with what did the reporter give you?"

"You mean the one you killed? She didn't give me anything."

"Stop the bullshit. Where's her photographer friend?"

"I don't know. Maybe the police can help you. I hear they're looking for him, too."

"Why did you call the police?"

"Duh...a dead body."

"You're a lying whore. I'm going to tear your place apart until I find what I want."

"There's nothing here."

Satchi slugs me hard in my face knocking me off balance. I fall to the ground. "There's more of the same if you don't tell me the truth."

"I've nothing to hide," I whimper struggling to stand. I'm seeing stars and my lip is bleeding.

As I rise, Satchi shoves me. I fall backwards narrowly missing the table edge. While I'm down, Satchi goes to the back door. I'm guessing he's letting his guys in, and this may be my only chance to get away. I get up and bolt out the front door. I pass the pizza guy who has just pulled up to the house. I throw him the money I still have crumpled in my fist. I warn him to take off. He doesn't seem to care for an explanation after he takes one look at my bruised and bleeding face.

I run to the police station and catch Detective Jones as he's leaving. He takes me to his office. I explain my bruises, Satchi's role in my injuries, and let him know I escaped as the rest of the gang was arriving. He gets me a wet cloth to clean my face.

After a while, Detective Jones accompanies me back to my place along with two other officers. I'm instructed to wait in the car while they check out the house. Their guns are out. A few minutes later the detective comes back outside and motions for me to come in.

"Brace yourself, Miss Moore. They tore your place apart."

Detective Jones did not exaggerate. Every room has been thoroughly ransacked from top to bottom. *Did they find Rob?*

"What were they looking for, Miss Moore?"

I shrug. "I presume it was those items I gave you earlier. I can't think of anything else of interest or value."

"They might return if they didn't find what they wanted. Do you have anywhere else to stay tonight?"

"Not really. Gus said I could stay with him in Indianapolis. However, there's no bus until tomorrow." *No way I'll stay with friends and possibly put them in harm's way.*

He sighs. "I'll have a squad car check on you periodically. Call 9-1-1 immediately if anyone comes. I'll call early tomorrow to verify your plans. I've checked the house. No one is here, and I locked the back door and checked the windows."

"Thanks, Detective. I won't take any chances. I'll call Gus and let him know I'm coming."

Detective Jones leaves. I lock the front door and turn straight into Rob's arms.

"I was so worried about you, and I see he hurt you. I should have come back inside. When I saw Satchi arrive, I stayed outside figuring the other guys would be coming, which they did. I saw you leave. Satchi let the rest of the guys in to help him toss the house. Are you okay?"

"I'm a little sore, nothing more."

"I saw you come back with Detective Jones."

"I told the detective I'm going to join Gus in Indianapolis tomorrow."

Rob says, "Good idea."

"What will you do?"

"I think it's time I rejoin the gang. I need answers."

Rob kisses me on the forehead, brings me in a bag of frozen peas for my face, and leaves to start our fire. After a while, I get some drinks and food. We settle on the couch and talk until midnight. There's a lull in our conversation.

We turn to each other, as if on cue, with desire in our eyes. I know I don't want to think any more. For now I only want to be totally with him. I stand and extend my hand to Rob. He takes it in his, and we go upstairs to my room, which is a disaster. We manage to find some space to stand. We begin undressing one another with growing passion. We fall on the mattress on the floor, wrapped in each other's arms.

Our lovemaking starts out slow, then grows to a fiery crescendo. I gasp with pleasure as he caresses and finally enters me. I never knew sex could be so sweet. Afterwards, we remain entwined, and fall asleep in each others' arms.

Chapter 10

Early the next morning, Detective Jones calls and checks on my travel plans. My bus leaves at 11 a.m., and I assure him I will be on it. I give Gus a quick call to let him know I'm coming. He sounds relieved and promises to pick me up at the bus station.

Rob and I have a leisurely breakfast. Reluctantly I leave him to shower, dress, and pack. We kiss good-bye and promise each other to be careful.

I arrive at the bus station with twenty minutes to spare. I just bought my ticket, when Detective Jones walks into the station.

"Detective, I'm surprised to see you. Is everything okay?"

"I wanted to make sure you're safe and to update you. I've been in touch with the photographer. John found Jessica's body before you did. He's safe and hiding, as he's petrified he's next on the killer's list."

The guy is smarter than me. "Does he have anything to help your investigation?"

"Actually, he has a lot I would like to have. He has pictures of the developer, the lobbyist, and the gang. Plus his camera records the audio of all the interviews Jessica conducted in the past three months. In short, he has more than she did."

"When will he get it to you?"

"I'm working out the arrangements. Right now he's focused on staying alive. Not having to worry about you or him will be a huge help."

The detective stays with me until I board the bus. I feel guilty not telling him about Rob, but my gut is telling me it's better to keep this relationship to myself for now.

***

Gus is waiting for me as I get off the bus in Indianapolis. He gives me a bear hug, which makes me feel instantly safe.

"You act like we haven't seen each other for a decade!" I laugh.

"Seems like it. What in the world happened to your face? I've been worried sick about you ever since you told me about poor Jessica. I'm so glad you're here and not in Shipley. Has something else happened?"

I fill Gus in on Satchi's visit, my home getting ransacked, and the photographer's conversation with Detective Jones.

Gus says, "It's even worse than I thought. Do you trust this detective?"

"I do. He seems to be trying to figure out our mess. I believe he's one of the good guys."

"Good to hear 'cause we sure could use a friend. One of the worst things about this nightmare is not knowing who we can trust."

"I know."

"Why did you let Satchi into your house?"

"I didn't. He just barged in. I'm petrified of the monster. Once I saw a chance to get away, I took it. By the looks of the mess they made of my place, there wasn't much they overlooked."

"Was anything taken?"

"Nothing I noticed. My guess is they were looking for Jessica's notes."

"I'm glad you called the police. You took quite a chance taking those things from her apartment. I bet the detective didn't like you withholding evidence."

I grimace. "No, he didn't. Luckily he decided to give me a break and not charge me."

"Did you find out anything from the notes?"

"Not really. Jessica was investigating ARX and had an appointment with a lobbyist this coming Thursday. She seemed to be running into a bunch of walls. Sound familiar? Bottom line is we still have no answers. Who and why are big unknowns. And those might not even be the right questions."

***

Gus's sister's home is about forty-five minutes from the bus station. It's a medium size red brick home in a well-established neighborhood with lots of large trees. He introduces me to his aunt. She looks frail but is awake and alert for a while but soon tires out. I follow Gus out to the kitchen.

"My aunt has difficulty swallowing, so I've been making soups and soft foods for her. Do you mind making a batch of instant pudding while I finish the soup? You'll find a bowl in the cupboard over there and a box of pudding on the counter. There's milk in the fridge."

"Sure thing."

We work in silence. It feels good being in the kitchen with Gus. It's a familiar routine allowing me to pretend all is right with our world, even if it's only for a few minutes.

While Gus feeds his aunt, I make lunch for us. In the afternoon he shows me the bedroom I will be using. It appears to belong to his niece. It's a lovely, feminine room done in lavender and cream. The furniture is a creamy French provincial. Her pictures display her friends and a love for the outdoors.

My cell phone rings. "Miss Moore?"

"Hello, Detective Jones. What can I do for you?"

"Is Mr. Breckman there? I'd like to talk with both of you."

"Yes, he downstairs. I'll go get him."

I find Gus on the couch in the living room. He has fallen asleep but is easily awakened.

I put the speaker on. "Okay, Detective. We're both here now."

"Hello, Mr. Breckman. Thanks for speaking with me."

Gus stretches as he responds, "Of course. What's up, Detective?"

"I'm calling to find out more about this developer, Jacob Reis. When did he first contact you?"

"It was about five or six weeks ago, maybe longer. I seem to be losing track of time."

"Did he come in person or was this on the phone?"

"In person. He talked with Alan and Joe the same day. I don't know if he talked with Amy, the lady who owns the gift shop on the other corner."

"Have you contacted her?"

"I don't have her cell phone number. Her sign says she's on vacation. Her shop's been closed this entire time. I'm not sure when she's coming back, but it should be soon. I've never known her to keep her shop closed for so long."

Jones pauses, then asks, "When was the last time you saw her?"

"I think it was a few days before the developer came in. I noticed her 'Gone on vacation' sign was up the day he was in my diner."

"Did the developer say why he wanted to purchase your businesses?"

Gus continues, "I never asked, but Alan did. He told Alan he intends to build deluxe condos there. None of us want to sell, and we don't understand who would be living in these ritzy units."

"But you did sell. Am I correct?"

"Yes, I decided it would be best after what happened to Alan and Joe. I want to leave before Suzanne or I get injured or worse. I don't want to sell, but I feel I've no choice."

I hold his hand for support. He appears to be on the verge of tears.

After a pause, Gus softly says, "Detective, my mother and father started our place in 1945. I grew up there. Once they retired, I took over. It's been my life, and one in which I've always taken great pride. I feel like I'm letting down the people who are most important to me-- my parents and Suzanne."

"I hear you. So far I can't link Reis with Satchi and his gang. There has to be a connection. I don't believe in coincidences. We tracked down the lobbyist, and he's agreed to come in tomorrow for questioning. We also arrested one of Satchi's gang."

"Which one?" I ask, fearing it's Rob.

"His name is Toby Laneer. Know him?"

"I'm not sure. Is he the tall, skinny one who wears a baseball cap or the stocky guy?" I ask.

"He's the tall one . We caught him breaking into your house, Miss Moore. I guess he was going back to be sure they hadn't missed anything."

"I'm glad you caught him, and I'm glad I wasn't there." *I wonder if Toby was looking for Rob. Where is Rob? Hope he's safe.*

"You both made the right decision to leave town. Can you stay until Monday?"

"My niece is due Saturday," Gus says.

"You're safer there than here. Toby isn't going anywhere for now, but the lobbyist is only here for questioning. We can't hold him. So, it's better you're away."

"What are you asking them?"

"I'm trying to connect the dots. Nothing is adding up. Please call if you decide to return to Shipley."

"Okay," we say in unison, and I hang up.

Gus and I stare at each other for a moment.

Breaking the silence, I say, "I wish they could arrest Satchi. I bet the gang would break up if he's gone."

"Yeah...I wonder why Toby went back to your place."

"Beats me. Why are they doing any of the things they've been doing? Jones is right. Nothing makes sense."

"Did you leave any travel plans around--this address or my cell number?"

"No, I carry those numbers in my phone which is always with me except when I sleep." A horrible thoughts hits me. My phone is on the nightstand at night. Rob could've accessed it either night. Do I need to worry? My instincts still say no.

"What's wrong? You look like you're a thousand miles away," says Gus.

"I...I guess everything is catching up with me. Do you need any help now?"

"No thanks. When my aunt wakes up around four, I'll give her another dose of medicine. Why don't you go up and get some rest."

"Sounds good. Call me if you need me."

I'm awakened about an hour later when I hear a text message alert on my phone. It's from Rob. He wants to know if I'm okay. He also says he misses me. I respond letting him know I'm okay. I tell him I miss him too. Then he tells me to delete the conversation.

I delete the text. *What if the group has nothing to do with the developer? Could Rob be the connection? To trust or not? I want to trust him, but...*

***

Around four in the afternoon, I go to the kitchen for a glass of water. I look in the living room, but Gus isn't there. I figure he's in with his aunt.

Not wanting to bother them, I settle on the couch. My phone rings a few minutes later. It's Rob.

"Have you decided when you're coming back?"

I know my answer won't please him. "We've decided to wait until Monday."

"That's probably a good idea, but I wish you'd come on Saturday." His tone is pleasant but a little subdued, like he doesn't want to be overheard.

I chuckle. "I miss you, too. But, there's no reason for Gus and I to rush back since he's not reopening the diner."

"I hate to admit it, but you are safer there. Keep in touch. Bye."

"Bye, Rob."

My thoughts are again on what the future holds for me. If I return to Shipley, what do I do next? Where will I work, and where will I live? Everything is changing.

Gus enters the living room. "You look lost in thought."

"Yeah, same old stuff. How's your aunt?"

"She seems okay. I gave her the meds and then read to her. She's sleeping now. In about an hour I'll take her some supper."

"Need any help?"

"I think I've got it under control. I made some soup and fixed some homemade applesauce for her. I've a chicken roasting for us."

"I'm feeling like a freeloader," I say.

"You're not. After cooking in the diner eight hours a day, six days a week, I'm used to it and it relaxes me."

"Have you reached any decisions on what you want to do next?"

Gus smiles and says, "Promise you won't laugh?"

I raise my right hand. "Never! What is it?"

"I've been looking into having a food truck. You know the kind, the truck parks at a business complex and sells coffee, juice, and pastries in the morning and light lunches at noon. A large town like Indianapolis has a lot of commercial sites with lots of hungry workers."

"What a great idea."

"Thanks. I'm starting small, as it will be some time before I make any profit."

"What made you decide on a food truck?"

"I've been kicking the idea around for several years. When all this trouble started, I talked with my sister who knew a guy who wants to sell his food truck business. He already has an established area, which I could take over. This way I can be close to the only family I have."

I smile at him. "Sounds perfect for you."

Gus nods, then says, "What're your plans?"

I sigh. "I don't know, yet. When you came in, I was thinking it's time to leave Shipley. There are too many painful memories and unpleasant people there."

"I hear you."

We sit in silence for a few minutes. *My future does look bleak at the moment.* Then I say, "It seems like I've always depended on others to take care of me."

"Any idea of what you want to do?"

I frown. "Hmm...I guess I'm one of those people with no imagination. I've always been grateful to have a job at the diner. I've never thought beyond it. The thought of leaving you and Gus's Place scares me."

"You're young. It will be a big change, but I think you're ready."

"Maybe so, but I don't know."

Gus hesitates. Then he says, "I never thought I'd say this, but losing the restaurant might turn out to be the best thing for both of us."

"Really? How so?"

"It's forcing us to move on. While you're here, why not check out the job market?"

"Maybe I will. Tell me more about your new business."

Smiling, Gus says, "I'm going to use the money from the sale of the diner plus the insurance money to buy the truck and the business. The seller is going to help me by financing what my down payment doesn't cover. I should be able to pay off the loan in two years. I need to get an Indiana food handling license. If you'll stay with my aunt tomorrow, I can get the paperwork started."

I nod and say, "Of course I will."

"Thanks. After I get back tomorrow, we need to concentrate on your career."

"Okay. I need all the help I can get. My mind is blank."

"You're probably still in shock after everything that's been happening. You have no holds in Shipley, right? So, why not here? We can remain friends, and my family will be your extended family."

"Sounds good. Let me think about it," I say as I stand and stretch. "Okay, enough talk about jobs. I feel like doing something. How about I make some veggies and biscuits to go with our chicken? I want a beer. How about you?

"Sounds good, but let me check on my aunt. I'll be right out."

My thoughts are racing. Moving to Indianapolis and starting a new life might be the answer. What about Rob? Since he revealed what he's really doing, I'm finding I like him more and more. I like how he treats me when we're alone, and I enjoy his sense of humor. I also think he's cute. Would I need to remain in Shipley? I don't know if I could unless the gang and all the problems disappear. Maybe he could move here, too. Whatever we do, we need to take it slow.

Chapter 11

Early the next morning, Gus heads out to work on getting a food license. His aunt falls asleep after her breakfast and morning medications. With nothing else to do, I get a cup of coffee and settle at the kitchen table. I realize I'm feeling sad, confused, and a little afraid. I'm a mess. I'm happy Gus has found a new career path. I can't begrudge him this new endeavor. If it hadn't been for his support after my parents and then my grandmother died, I don't know what I would have done. I'm realizing my anchor is the emotional support Gus provides, not his restaurant.

My phone rings. "Hello, Miss Moore. Is everything okay on your end?"

"Yes, Detective. Gus and I are safe and sound. Any news?"

"Did Miss Keyes tell you about the access road and the possibility of a casino and entertainment complex building here?"

"Yeah, she did. Is Toby Laneer still in jail."

"No, his attorney got him released on bail. The extortion business must be doing well."

"Not funny, Detective."

"Sorry, Miss Moore, I'm not taking this lightly."

I pause. "I'm still confused. What does all this have to do with the reporter getting killed.?"

"We're still working on it."

"Is there anything I can do?"

"No, this is police business. I called to find out if you are still returning to Shipley on Monday."

"I'm not sure. Gus has decided to buy a food truck business here in Indianapolis. He only needs to return to pack and to attend the closing next Friday, and I need to get my stuff, too."

"Okay. The longer you stay away, the safer you'll be. Let me know when you'll be returning."

"Will do. Bye." *I need to move someplace else, away from all the craziness. I'll have to contact a real estate agent to sell my home. And, I need to get a job. Hey, look at me making plans!*

When Gus returns, he seems excited. He reports being successful in starting the process to get an Indiana food vendors license.

"You look happy," I say as he joins me in the kitchen.

"These last few weeks have gotten me down. But now, I'm excited to get this new business up and running. It's giving me something to think about besides the extortion and suffering of my friends." He pours a cup of coffee and sits with me at the table.

"What are you going to call your new business?"

Gus grins. "What do you think of, "Gus's Deli Wagon'?"

"Perfect."

"Thanks. A long time ago I began kicking around what I was going to do when I retired. Nothing appealed to me. Then I realized, I don't want to retire. I needed a change, so now I'm going on wheels."

"I'm surprised you never mentioned this to me before." I remark.

Gus shrugs. "With the extortion and the violence, I was forced to move ahead a little faster than planned. When my sister hooked me up with this fellow getting ready to sell his business, it felt right."

"By the way, Detective Jones called," I say as I refill my glass of water.

"Anything new?"

"Not much. The lobbyist is working for ARX, a casino, and some sort of entertainment group. Toby, the gang member, hired a lawyer and is out of jail. No answers. The detective thinks we should extend our stay here. What do you think of waiting until closing?" I ask.

"I'm way ahead of you. I already contacted my niece about our staying longer. She's in complete agreement."

"Great. We'll have a chance to work on our futures. Have you contacted Cheryl?'

"Not yet, but it's time. I'll go call her before my aunt needs attention."

"Okay. I'll be in my room if you need me."

Soon after I get to my bedroom, I get a call from Rob. "Are you okay?"

"Yeah, we're fine. Has something happened?"

"Satchi is furious with you."

I shrug. "Is it because Toby was arrested? The police caught him. I had nothing to do with it. Besides, he's already out on bail."

"I know, but you can never predict how Satchi will react. I'm keeping close to these guys so they don't try to go to Indianapolis. I guess I'll see you Monday."

"Uh...now we're not returning until Friday, when Gus closes on the diner."

"Well, let me know. I miss you. Bye." Rob sounds down.

When I hang up, I suddenly feel the weight of all the decisions I have to make on my own.

***

On Friday, Gus goes to the hospital to visit his sister. I busy myself with cleaning and laundry. Late morning I get another text from Rob. He says he wants to see me.

I reply I'll see him Friday.

He answers he can't wait. He asks to come here.

I text that's not a good idea. What if the gang follows him. I ask him to try to be patient and understand. Gus and his family do not deserve to be a part of this nightmare. I tell him again I will see him on Friday. *All I need is for Rob to bring those goons here. Maybe it's time to tell Detective Jones and Gus about Rob.* I don't delete the text. I call the detective and leave a voicemail. This is the right thing to do.

At eleven o'clock I give Gus's aunt her medications and read to her until she falls asleep. Gus comes home shortly after noon. He takes lunch in to his aunt and comes back to the kitchen a little while later. He joins me at the table where I have set out lunch.

"How is your sister doing?" I ask.

"Much better. She's awake and alert. They moved her out of the I.C.U. The doctor thinks she'll be able to come home in about a week."

"That's great."

"Sure is. Anything happen here while I was gone?"

The time is right to tell Gus about Rob, but I can't seem to find the words.

"I left a message for the detective to call. I want to let him know we'll be returning next Friday."

"Isn't it unusual for him not to return your call right away?"

"Yeah, it is. I hope nothing has happened."

We look at each other. Neither of us want to think the worst, but it's hard not to.

When I return to my room, I notice a text came in from Rob checking if I am angry with him.

I respond I am being cautious.

He says he can get away without those guys following him. He pleads for me to consent to let him come here.

I'm getting irritated with his persistence. I write I don't want to take a chance and to please leave me alone.

I don't delete this conversation either. By the time I go to bed, the detective still has not returned my call. Rob seems to be pressing hard to know my return date, and Satchi is furious with me and blames me for Toby's arrest. Has this situation taken a turn for the worse?

***

I toss and turn most of the night. The pieces aren't making any sense, and I keep feeling like I'm missing something. It's driving me nuts not having any definite answers. The next morning I awaken with an idea.

Gus is eating breakfast when I enter the kitchen. "Good morning, Suzanne."

"Good morning. How's your aunt doing today?" I grab a bowl and spoon and join him at the table. I help myself to the cereal and milk already there.

"She had a good night and ate a good breakfast. She's already fallen back asleep."

"Good. We have time to talk. I have an idea I want to run by you." I take a spoonful of cereal.

Gus tilts his head. "I'm listening."

"What if we're on the wrong track about this sale? What if the real reason to get these specific shops is because of the property itself?"

"We already know they want it as a building site. So what?"

"What if it's not the primary reason? Think about it. Even if the developer wants to build something, why the big rush? Plus, why didn't he approach the shops across the street? They would have given him the same size lot on which to build."

"You're right about the size and location, but what other reason could there be?"

"I'm looking for anything different or unique about these properties."

Gus scratches his head as he thinks over my question. "Amy's place was once offices for doctors. My place was a clinic. Joe and Alan's shops were a lawyer's office and a jewelry store."

"That's interesting. I never knew their original uses."

"Oh yeah, and there's a tunnel running under all the buildings on this block."

"A tunnel? I wonder what it was used for."

Gus shrugs. "I don't know. Maybe to get from one building to the next without going outside."

"I can't shake the feeling the developer has a hidden agenda."

"Like what?"

"I don't know. Were there ever any stories about what went on in the tunnel?"

"I never heard any rumors."

"Did you ever explore the tunnels?"

Gus rubs the back of his neck. "No I didn't, because my father blocked off our entrances to them when we moved in. He hated the dirt basement, so he never used it and neither have I. Don't really need it with the large pantry upstairs."

"Did he ever talk about finding anything in the tunnels before he blocked them?"

"I don't think so. Any ideas?"

"Oh, I don't know. Maybe he saw evidence of something buried or some kind of wrongdoing."

"I think there was only trash down there. Oh, wait, I almost forgot. He found a picture taken in 1919 of the Cincinnati Reds." Gus smiles as recalls the memory. "That year was the first time the Reds won the World Series. My dad was thrilled to find it, because he was a huge fan."

"Oh yeah, I remember that picture. You have it hanging over your desk at the diner."

"I did, now it's hanging in my room here. I love this photo because I remember how happy it made my dad. Sorry, no rumors of buried treasure or dead bodies. I remember he said the picture was dusty but nothing about it being buried."

"Wouldn't it be wild if it's something hidden in the frame?"

"Highly unlikely since both my dad and I have handled it countless times. But, the tunnels are intriguing. There has to be some reason the developer is so gung ho on getting these properties."

"Who was the original owner?"

"I have no idea. All these buildings were built before 1920."

"Do you think Alan or Joe might remember something?"

"They might. I'll give them a call and ask. I need to see how they're doing anyway."

"Okay, and I'll research the real estate info to see if I can find the name of the original owner. I need to call Detective Jones again. He never did return my call from yesterday. I'll tell him what we're working on." I reach for my phone and tap in his number. I again leave a voicemail. *Rats, I'm ready to confess my relationship with Rob, and now I can't find him.*

I carry Gus's laptop to my bedroom and begin the search. I quickly find the sales reports of all four properties. What's interesting is all the businesses were originally owned by the Diamond Star Group. However, it must have been some kind of trust, because I can't find the names of the people in the group. I'll need help finding their identities. Maybe the newspaper will have some helpful information in their archives. Or maybe there's nothing to find. I really want to explore those tunnels. I can't believe I never knew they existed.

My phone rings. It's Detective Jones. "Miss Moore, you wanted me to call?"

"Yes, thank you. I'm relieved to hear from you. I was getting worried."

"Didn't mean to cause any concern. I ran into some problems while I was in Columbus. What can I help you with today?"

Now's the time to tell him. Is it the right thing to do?

"Miss Moore?"

Right or wrong, I make my decision. "Sorry, Detective, I haven't been completely honest with you."

"Have you withheld information again? I warned you." He sounds irritable.

"I've become friendly with Rob, one of the gang members. We've been keeping it secret. Rob said it was safer for both of us."

"You're seeing one of the gang? The same group extorting money and terrorizing all of you?"

I grimace. "Sounds awful when you say it like that."

"How else can I put it?"

"It just happened. Rob kept coming around. He's always sweet to me when we're alone. There's something different about him." *I'm afraid to tell him Rob's working undercover for fear the wrong guy will hear about it. Rob needs to reveal this information.*

"What do you mean 'different'?"

"I know his loyalties aren't with Satchi, as he's hiding stuff from the gang. And, he seems to spend a lot of time away from those guys."

"Any idea who this someone else might be?"

"Maybe Reis, especially if Satchi and crew aren't working for him."

"Interesting but worthless without proof. What's Rob's last name?"

"King."

"Any of his DNA in your house?"

"Fingerprints should be everywhere, and there may be beer bottles in my kitchen trashcan."

"Already checked. Somebody did a good job of cleaning."

"Damn. Well, I do have another idea."

"What?"

"What if the developer is interested in these properties for some unknown reason?"

"Go on."

"Well, I don't know. But, it's strange how the developer is only going after these particular shops."

"Let me know if you find out anything. And, Miss Moore, don't withhold any more information from me. I've got a job to do, and you're getting in my way."

"Okay, Detective. One more thing before you hang up."

I sense he's losing patience with me by his terse response. "What?"

"Please don't tell Gus about Rob. I need to do it."

"If I remember. Good-bye, Miss Moore."

I breathe a sigh of relief. Even though the detective is less than happy with me, he's alive and knows about Rob. One down and one to go. Gus will be harder to tell. I dread his disappointment in me.

My phone rings. It's Rob. "Suzanne, what's going on?"

"Why are you calling me? I asked you to leave me alone."

"I'm calling to find out what I've done to upset you."

"I told you I'm not upset. We're taking this slow, remember? Please be patient."

"I thought we cared for each other."

"We'll have plenty of time to work on our relationship once all these problems get resolved. You need to focus on getting your evidence for the Hoskins. I told Detective Jones about us, but I didn't mention your P.I. work."

"Thanks for not revealing my undercover work. I still don't know who we can trust. I wish we could talk in person. Bye for now." Rob sounds sincere.

"Bye." I hang up, turn off my phone, and wish my heart would follow my head. All I want to do is call him back. I remind myself I was the one asking for space. To stop temptation, I grab the laptop, leave the phone on the bed, and go downstairs.

I begin researching newspaper stories from 1918 to 1947. I'm so glad I live in a small town with a small paper. Even so, it'll take a lot of time to read through all these editions.

Gus rejoins me. "Talked with both Alan and Joe."

"Did they remember anything?"

"Alan remembers hearing a story about one of the doctors getting murdered in his office."

"Wow, I wonder when that happened. Did he remember the year?"

"No, but by the time my parents started the diner, the end unit was empty. Agnes and her daughter moved in around 1960."

"Agnes is older than you?"

"Yeah, she was the same age as my parents."

"Odd. She sure doesn't look over fifty."

"You're thinking of Amy. She's the granddaughter. My guess is she's somewhere around thirty-five."

I laugh. "Oh, I see. I guess I never met Agnes or her daughter. I wonder where Amy has been. She's missing all the fun."

"Yeah, lucky her."

While Gus goes in to spend time with his aunt, I continue going through the online articles. Twenty-five years of papers. An hour into my search I find a story about a bank robbery in downtown Shipley. The robber was shot by the bank guard but got away. Three days later there is another story about a doctor who was found dead in his office. He'd been stabbed. Both articles said there were ongoing investigations being conducted. I'm unable to find a follow-up.

Gus returns to the living room. "Any luck with your research?"

I tell him what I discovered. "So far I've found no information to help us understand what's going on now."

"You think the two incidents are related?"

"I do. Specifically I think the robber and the murderer were the same person. He was shot, went to the doctor's office for help, and then killed the doctor to get rid of a witness."

"Makes sense. The bank and the doctor's office were only two blocks apart."

"So far I haven't found where they ever apprehended the bank robber."

We both are quiet for a few minutes.

I break the silence. "What if the robber killed the doctor and took off through the tunnel with the money?"

"Go on." Gus leans forward in his chair.

"Say he had to stash the money in the tunnel thinking he'd come back later to get it, but he never made it back. Maybe he buried it so no one else could get it. Maybe the developer would like to get his hands on the money left behind."

"How much was taken?"

"Newspaper estimated around thirty thousand dollars."

Gus shakes his head and frowns. "Thirty thousand was a lot of money back in the twenties, but I can't see the same amount making these properties so attractive today."

"True. I wonder if any of this connects to Reis or ARX?"

"Sounds pretty far-fetched to me. I'm going to take in my aunt's supper. I feel like some Chinese food tonight. How about you?"

"Sounds good. What can I do?"

"Call in our order. The menu and the restaurant's phone number are on the board behind the phone. I'd like orange chicken, fried rice, and two eggrolls. Get whatever you want. I'll pick it up in about an hour."

"Will do." After I phone in our order, I go upstairs to freshen up. When I return to the kitchen, Gus is just leaving. I set the table. Suddenly I realize I'm not alone.

"I thought Gus would never leave."

"Rob!" I gasp as I turn toward him, not knowing whether to be happy or alarmed.

He gives me a hesitant smile. "I just wanted to see you."

"This isn't cute. Who came with you?" I say as I look behind him.

"No one. Satchi and group are back in Shipley."

I frown. "Aren't you taking a chance going off on your own? Doesn't Satchi get suspicious? Did you ever consider he could be on to you?"

"He's not. Forget those guys. I know what I'm doing. You sounded different. I felt I should check it out."

This man is exasperating. "I asked you to give me space. You're putting Gus and his family in harm's way. You shouldn't be here."

"I want you to understand I'm on your side. I guess I'm as confused as you are about all this mess. I'm used to working alone, but I feel we have a bond. We're in this together. I needed to talk to you in person. Try to believe me."

"I do believe you. I feel a connection too, but we need to take a step back. It's hard to think when you get emotional. This relationship has caught us both by surprise. We'll figure it out, but not here. Please go."

"You're right, and I'm sorry if I scared you. We are in this together, and I need to do my part."

Rob grabs me imparting his feelings through the intensity of his kiss. I find myself clutching him and kissing him with my own passion. Then he's gone. I'm still standing in a daze a few minutes later when Gus returns.

"Grab us some beers. Let's eat, I'm starved," he says as he starts pulling cartons from the sacks.

Although this might be the ideal time to tell Gus about Rob, I can't do it. I chicken out again. The rest of the evening is quiet, and I go to bed early.

Chapter 12

Elle, Gus's niece, comes in around noon the next day. She asks Gus to set up a temporary bedroom in the den, but we had anticipated her request and arranged it all before she arrived. Elle wants to stay close to her great aunt. She's thirty-eight and lives in Chicago. She has a job as a hotel concierge. She's tall and has a striking figure. Gus and Elle seem to have a close relationship. Her first day here she spends most of her time with her great aunt. In the evening I hear her and Gus talk long into the night.

After breakfast on Sunday, Gus tells me Elle thinks we should explore the tunnels. We're all in agreement our time is running out due to the closing scheduled for Friday.

"Great idea. Should we ask Detective Jones to join us?" I ask.

"Since we're only going to be there for the day, why don't we call him if we find anything? Or were you thinking we need protection?"

"More the latter, but also to make sure if we find any money it gets into the right hands. Maybe there's a finder's reward," I say with a grin quickly changing to a frown. "Or maybe there's nothing to find."

"Who knows? Let's do it anyway. I'll borrow my aunt's car."

"Do you think the developer would back out of buying if we find the money?"

Gus shrugs. "I still think the amount is too trifling for him. But if he does back out, it wouldn't be the worst news. I could put it on the market and maybe get a better price."

"Okay then, we have a plan. I'm tired of sitting around waiting for other people to figure out what's going on. I can get some more of my things while we're there."

"Me too," says Gus.

***

Late the next morning we arrive at the diner. Gus parks in the rear, so we won't attract any unwanted attention. Armed with a shovel, a hammer, and flashlights, we make our way to the basement. We decide to explore the tunnel connecting Gus's Place to the hardware store. Our logic is this section is shorter and would have made a good hiding spot away from the doctors' offices. However, the entrance is a dead end.

I groan. "Wow, when your dad blocked off the entrances, he meant business."

We are looking at a cement block wall. Our little tools don't even make a dent. We had expected a boarded up entrance, not this barricade.

As Gus wipes his brow from all the effort, he says, "I wonder if Joe blocked his entrance."

"Give him a call. Do you think it's safe to enter?"

"I don't see why not." Gus calls Joe and is given permission to go into the store. His son will meet us there in a half hour.

"Have you checked out your own basement?"

"No, but there shouldn't be anything down here. Feel free to look around."

As he predicted, the search proves fruitless.

When we walk up the stairs, we find Satchi and his tag-a-longs waiting in the kitchen. There's no way to escape.

Satchi sneers at us and says, "Well, old man, what did you find?"

I nervously lick my lips and respond, "Nothing. We're just trying to be sure Gus doesn't leave anything behind." I'm relieved we left the shovel and other equipment downstairs.

Satchi snaps back, "Shut up, bitch. I wasn't talking to you."

Gus moves his hands up and down in a calming motion. "Satchi, take it easy. She told you the truth."

Satchi grabs Gus by his throat and slams him against the wall. "It better be."

Rob goes up beside them. "Chill, Satchi."

"Stay out of it," Satchi snarls.

Rob shrugs and says, "Just saying. We came to find out if the diner is reopening."

Satchi turns back to Gus and says, "What about it? Are you reopening this dump?"

Angry, Gus snaps back. "No, you made sure of that."

Satchi smashes his fist into Gus's face. Blood begins to gush from his nose as the gang turns and marches out.

I rush to Gus. "Are you all right?"

"I think he might have broken my nose." He's covered in blood.

I find a towel for him. Luckily the freezer is still running, and I find a small package of vegetables to press to his face.

"Let's go to the ER."

"No, I'll be okay. Besides, it's almost time to go next door."

I shake my head at his stubbornness. "Satchi is a psychopath."

"Yeah, he's totally out of control," Gus responds while washing his face and hands at the sink.

We walk over to meet Joe's son, who agrees with me Gus needs to see a doctor. But Gus is too excited to see what we might find. There's no barricade on this side. The tunnel has a dirt floor and is surprisingly dry. We can stand upright, and it's wide enough for two abreast. Unfortunately, the tunnel is dark and full of nothing but cobwebs.

"We might as well go back to Indianapolis," Gus says as we return to the street.

"Yeah, since we can't get into the other side. Is it okay with you if I go home first and pack up more of my things? If you don't feel up to it, it's okay."

"No, I'm fine. I'll drop you off at your place, and then I'll come back and pack up more from my apartment. I need to start inventorying the kitchen to see what I can use for the food truck."

"Do you think we're safe separating?"

"Yeah, I think they're done for the day. They just wanted to be sure we hadn't found anything."

***

After I arrive, I walk slowly through my house. It's a mess and matches my thinking. Grabbing my large duffel bag, I go upstairs to pack my clothes and whatever else can be crammed in. Towels and bedding go in some smaller bags. When all the bags are full, I drag them downstairs. I'm carrying the last one, when I find Rob waiting at the bottom of the stairs.

"Are you spying on me again?"

Rob smiles and says, "Trade secrets."

"You can wipe off the grin. Satchi hurt Gus."

Rob reaches out to take the bag and says, "I know, and I'm sorry. Satchi's unstable. Moving someplace?"

"Yes," I say as I turn to go back up for a final check.

"Where to? Indianapolis?" Rob follows me.

"Far from here and all of them." I begin checking dresser drawers and the closet for any remaining items.

"Where?"

From inside the closet I say, "Don't know yet."

"Don't know or won't tell me?"

"I haven't made any definite plans, since I don't know where I'll find a job," I say as I come out.

Rob places his hands on my shoulders. "You will let me know where you go, right?"

I look up at him say, "Of course I will. But, I need time to get my life in order. By the way, where's Satchi? Gus is alone at the diner."

"No problem. Satchi's done for the day. The gang's back at his place getting drunk."

"Good. We don't need any more drama."

Rob sighs. "I better get going. I'm sorry Gus was hurt. Be safe." He gently kisses me on the cheek and leaves.

I sit on the bottom step to wait for Gus. I'm sure I'm making the right choice going away from Shipley.

I hear two honks. Gus has arrived. I grab my duffel bag and open the front door.

"Let me get this one for you." Gus walks up to the porch and takes the big bag and heads back to the car.

"I hope you feel better than you look, Gus." His eyes are bruised looking and his nose is swollen.

"I'll live." Gus chuckles as he tosses my stuff into the trunk.

I make a couple more trips for the smaller bags and boxes of food and all sorts of miscellaneous items I tell myself I can't live without.

I feel a sense of relief as we drive away. I didn't realize how tense I was.

Gus says, "Sad to be leaving Shipley?"

"Yes and no. I don't like feeling scared all the time, but it makes me sad being forced to leave a place I love."

"I know, but it's not our sweet little town anymore."

"Did you talk with Detective Jones? Does he know Satchi attacked you? Do you think your nose is broken?"

Gus gingerly touches it. "I'm sore, but I know it's not broken. I didn't call the detective as I don't want to press charges. I want them to get Satchi on a bigger charge. These guys have a good attorney and get out much too quickly. It seems like we're on the right track, though, judging by their curiosity."

"Yeah, but what track? We're running out of time. I'm still going to call Jones and tell him about our trip to town." *And when Gus isn't around, I'll tell him about my unexpected visit with Rob.*

***

After hearing our report, Jones says, "I understand Gus wanting to nail Satchi with as many charges as he can, but this attack shouldn't be ignored. We could at least try to lock him up until his court date."

Gus has been listening. "Okay, Detective, I'll file assault charges. What do I have to do? Can I sign any paperwork from here at my sister's home?"

"No. Come back into town tomorrow to sign the paperwork. Then we can pick him up."

In unison we say, "Okay."

After hanging up, I say, "I think you're doing the right thing. I'll go with you as a witness."

"I hate to admit it, but Satchi scares me. He'll be angry. If he makes bail like the other guy did, we could be in for a lot of trouble."

"What about Alan and Joe? Do you think they'd be able to make statements against him?"

"I'll call them and find out," Gus says as he pulls out his phone.

Before he calls, I ask, "Do you have a sledge hammer? We could use it to bust through the other entrance."

"Yeah, I have one. But I'm not staying in town long enough to use it, unless they put Satchi in jail."

Chapter 13

The following day we drive the two-hour trip back to Shipley to sign the paperwork filing charges against Satchi. Detective Jones is waiting for us. We tell him Alan and Joe want to add their complaints, since nothing was done the first time. Detective Jones says he'll take their statements, but the arrest has to be on Gus's incident. As soon as Gus signs, Detective Jones leaves. He says he'll call us once Satchi is apprehended. We decide we'll wait in the police station. Neither one of us is feeling brave enough to go to the diner until he's arrested.

About an hour later, the detective calls. They have Satchi. He warns us Satchi is calling for an attorney and could make bail as early as tomorrow. We tell the detective about our plans to go into the other side of the tunnel. He advises us to be quick and to let him know if we find anything. He reminds us the rest of the gang are still out there.

Gus and I rush to the diner. We go downstairs, and Gus works on the opening between his place and the gift shop. I feel guilty watching him do all the work with the sledgehammer. After many swings, a tired, sweaty Gus starts to get an opening large enough for us to enter. We grab our flashlights and begin. This is a longer segment, but it's exactly like the other side--dry, wide, and dark. However, we're bombarded with a horrible odor.

"Whew, what stinks?" I ask trying to wave it away.

Gus puts his handkerchief to his nose and says, "I'm not sure. Smells like a dead animal or something."

We make our way about forty feet into the tunnel where we find a human skeleton and see a satchel next to the body. Gus insists we leave it alone and get out. He has to shake me as I'm horrified by this sight. Between the smell and this sight, I feel nauseous as I turn and follow Gus.

Once we're in the restaurant section, I call Detective Jones to let him know about our findings. He tells us to stay upstairs and wait for him, since it's now a crime scene. I'm surprised by his response, but we follow his orders.

We sit at the counter to wait. We don't turn on the lights, we don't want to advertise our presence to any of the gang.

When the detective arrives, he's accompanied by the medical examiner and two police officers.

Jones comes over to us while the other three go downstairs. "Mr. Breckman, Miss Moore, did you see anything else while in the tunnel?"

Gus responds, "We saw a bag or suitcase of some kind next to the skeleton. We left as soon as we saw it, and we didn't touch anything. Also, there's an awful odor in there."

"Okay, and you didn't remove anything?"

Together we respond, "No."

"We're investigating the situation here. You should go back to Indianapolis. Satchi will definitely make bail, and I don't want you two around when he gets out."

We need no convincing and leave for Indianapolis.

***

Early the next morning we call the detective. I put the call on speaker.

"The skeleton appears old judging by what's left of the clothing. The M.E. will know more later."

I ask, "Did you find anything else in the tunnel?"

"Yes, we did, but I'm not at liberty to say anything more as it's an ongoing investigation."

Gus frowns and asks, "If it's an ongoing investigation, will I still be able to move forward with the sale on Friday?"

"No, the closing will be delayed by court order. Stay in touch with the title company for any info on a future date."

I ask, "Do you think we found the robber's skeleton?"

"It's too soon to say. Don't come back to town without letting me know."

What else was discovered? Was it connected to the bad smell? Gus and I mull this over after the call.

"How do you feel about postponing the closing?"

Gus sighs. "I don't know. I need the sale to move forward with the food truck, but I don't want Reis to win. I want this nightmare to be over, but I have a bad feeling about what they found down there."

"Yeah, I know what you mean. I wonder how long we'll have to wait before we find out what it was."

Gus stands and stretches. "I know I need to keep busy or this tension will drive me crazy. What have you done about getting a new job? Will you be staying in Indianapolis?"

I shrug. "I haven't done anything yet. I don't know what I should pursue. I promise I won't end up being a freeloader. Please be patient with me."

Gus squeezes my shoulder and says, "You got it. Now, my sister is due to get out of the hospital as early as next Wednesday. She won't be able to do steps for a while, so the den bedroom will be perfect for her. Elle has to get back to work, and she'll be gone before her mom comes home. If you're here, you can help me take care of my Aunt Ann and Shirley. It'll give all of you a chance to get to know each other."

I smile. "Thanks, I'll be happy to help."

"I plan to stay here until my sister makes a complete recovery. Then I'll get my own place. You are welcome to do the same."

After dinner I borrow his laptop again. With Elle's help, I start browsing a couple employment sites. I spend a few hours reviewing the posted jobs and submit my resume to a few. To be honest, nothing interests me.

Chapter 14

Gus calls the title company the next day. The sale is definitely on hold by court order.

I say, "Sorry about the delay."

"It may not be a problem. I have some good news to share. The seller of the food truck has agreed to wait this out. As soon as I receive the insurance money, I'll use it as the down payment. Once the sale goes through, I'll be able to get my inventory stocked. I'm still waiting for all my paperwork to get processed, since I can't do anything until I get it."

I clap my hands together. "I'm happy for you."

"Yeah, it's a relief to know I can move forward despite this latest complication."

I decide to share my thoughts with him. "I'm curious to find out if the detective has any updates."

Gus nods. "You mean like what's in the bag?"

"Exactly, and what was causing the smell."

Gus grimaces. "I'm almost afraid to find out what that was. I also wonder how Reis is taking the delay."

"I think if the findings arc unrelated to his reason for buying, he might just be impatient. However, he might be sweating if he's done something he shouldn't. Do you still plan on selling if he withdraws his offer?"

"Yeah, that's my plan."

***

The next day I again search the internet for job listings and find one for a local truck stop. They're looking for a night manager. I make a call and set up an interview for this afternoon. Gus thinks it's a great fit for me and lets me borrow his aunt's car.

After the interview, I stop at a local branch of my bank. I inquire about the criteria for a business loan. Maybe I could buy my own diner somewhere. Of course, it might be a waste of time, but there's no harm in trying. I take the application with me.

In the evening I get a call from the truck stop. I run downstairs to let Gus know I got the job and will be starting in a week.

"Terrific. You can work and save some money until you figure out what you really want to do."

"How did you know this wasn't it?"

"Come on, I know you better than that."

"I don't know what I'd do without you." I pat his arm. "Hey, where's Elle? I want to thank her for her help."

"She's in with her grandmother. My aunt isn't doing well. Her congestive heart failure appears to be worse. She's on oxygen now, but the doctor warned us she may have to go to the hospital."

"I'm so sorry. Can I do anything for you guys?"

"It's in God's hands now. She's a sweet woman. I know it's killing my sister to not be with her."

"I can imagine. I'll keep you all in my prayers."

"I hope you don't mind, but I want to go sit with her and Elle."

"Of course. I'll go back to my bedroom. Please let me know if I can do anything."

As I reenter my room, Rob calls.

I ask, "Why are you calling? I thought we agreed to wait."

"Yeah, we did. But, I wanted to see if you know what happened at the diner? Both the diner and the gift shop are taped off and being guarded by the police."

"We found a skeleton in the tunnel between the two stores."

"Tunnel?"

"There's a tunnel running under the shops."

"Whose skeleton did they find?"

"I don't know, but I think it might be the guy who robbed the bank back in the late twenties. I don't know much else."

"There's definitely something going on."

"What do you mean?"

"Satchi, Toby, and Luke left town as soon as Satchi made bail."

"Where'd they go? What about the other two?"

"The three went to Columbus. The other two guys were arrested and taken to Stockton, where they had outstanding warrants."

"Wow, the old gang is falling apart. Of course, it's always been a strange group. It's more like a bunch of hired thugs. So, when do you leave?"

Rob is silent.

"Have you been kicked out of this fine group of goons?"

No response.

"Well, have a nice life..."

"Wait, are you back in Indianapolis?"

I hesitate. "Yeah."

"You'll be safe there. When are you coming back?"

"I'm not sure. I've taken a job here."

"When can we get together?"

"I have to come back to sell my house. We'll talk then."

"Please be careful. Bye for now."

I have a head full of questions and a troubled heart. I toss and turn for what seems like hours. *What else was found in the tunnel? Why did those guys go to Columbus? If Satchi is gone, is Rob's undercover work over? Arghh, these questions without answers are making me crazy.*

***

In the morning I wake up with a plan. Why not go home and finish packing and cleaning up my house? Satchi and his thugs are gone, and

115

Rob may or may not be around. Go today and come back Sunday in plenty of time to start my job Monday night.

While Gus and I eat breakfast, I tell him about my plans.

His reaction comes quickly. "How can you be sure Satchi is gone?"

"The detective mentioned it." I'm lying again.

"We're taking my aunt to the hospital this morning. Elle and I'll be staying all day. I was feeling bad leaving you here alone. But, now you'll be busy. The only thing worrying me is Satchi could come back at any time, and you'll be alone."

"Yeah, I know, so I'll alert Detective Jones of my plans. Please don't worry. You guys have enough on your plate as it is."

"I can't help worrying."

Hugging Gus I go back up to pack. I call the detective, and Elle and Gus drop me off at the bus station on their way to the hospital. There's a two-hour wait. My phone buzzes, it's a text message from Rob.

"Satchi still gone. Please come for weekend."

It's like he read my mind. I text, "On my way. Need to close up house. Jones aware I'll be in town."

His response, "Great!"

The bus finally arrives, and the drive seems long. Not being able to concentrate on my book, I begin to think about my new job. One immediate goal is to increase the cleanliness of the place. The restaurant looked messy when I was there for my interview, but I can easily organize routine cleanings of the kitchen and restaurant areas.

***

Walking the few blocks to my house, I notice the town is eerily quiet. The police still have the diner and the gift shop taped off. There's a police car in front of the buildings. Unfortunately, the detective has given us no updates. The new date for closing has not been set. I've had no word about my application for the loan. I'm keeping my fingers crossed it'll be approved, and Gus will sell the diner. Then life will be perfect for both of us.

When I enter my house, I feel overwhelmed. What a mess. I'll be working my butt off to get this place back in order so it'll look good when I put it on the market. While I eat the carry-out dinner bought on my way here, I start making a to-do list.

I hear Rob come in. *My reason for returning has arrived.*

"Welcome home." He leans down and kisses my cheek.

"I hoped you'd show up."

"Miss me? I missed you."

I smile up at him. "Yes, I missed you."

"This house is a wreck. What would you like me to do to help you?"

"I've started a list. Here, take a look." I slide my list over to Rob.

He looks it over and whistles. "Looks like we'll be busy."

"You do know you don't have to help me."

"I know. I want to help. I see you've already eaten, but I haven't. I'll order a pizza. Do you have any beer?"

I nod and point at the refrigerator.

After he calls in the order, Rob starts on the kitchen. I go upstairs and work on packing the hall closet. Even with all the things I packed before, there is still so much to go over. The pizza arrives, and we take a break while Rob eats. I open beers for both of us.

Between bites, Rob says, "So, you're definitely leaving Shipley?"

"Yeah."

"Why?"

"Since the findings in the tunnel, I applied for a business loan. I'd like to buy my own place but not here. There are too many problem people."

"Is Gus okay with selling his place? What if Reis backs off?"

"Gus wants to stay in Indianapolis. He's in the process of buying a food truck business. He's very excited about the whole thing. And, I can't tell you how good it is to see him happy again. This extortion situation and all the violence has really gotten him down. He's ready to leave Shipley, too."

"He wants to stay in Indianapolis?"

"Yeah, he wants to stay close to his sister. He's going to live with her until she recovers from her accident."

"What will you do if you don't get the loan?"

"No matter what happens, I'll sell the house. I need to move somewhere with more restaurants for better job possibilities."

"I imagine it's hard to sell your family home."

I nod, then shrug. "I need the money to support myself whatever happens. I can't afford not to sell. It'll be hard, but what else can I do?"

Rob stands up and begins clearing the mess on the table. "I hear you. I guess it's time to get back to work."

"You don't have to stay."

"I know I don't have to, but I want to be with you. Now go upstairs before I jump you right here on the kitchen table."

I laugh as I climb the stairs. I finish the hall closet and begin working on the other two guest bedrooms. I'm partially done with the second one, when Rob joins me.

"How's it going up here?"

"Great. I'm making a lot of progress. Do you like my stacks? I have one for items I want to keep, one to give away, and the rest is going to be thrown out."

"Very efficient. I'm proud of you for keeping so little."

"Me, too. I only want my favorite mementoes and things I can still use. Besides, I already took over a load."

Rob smiles at me. "What do you say we knock off for the night?"

"I am tired, and sleep sounds good."

"Sleep is not exactly what I had in mind," Rob says, as he takes my hand and begins to pull me toward my bedroom.

"Mmm...I like your thinking."

"Shh." He begins to kiss me and pull off my clothes. All thought gone, I begin kissing and disrobing him. I give into the erotic feelings his tongue and hands are arousing. We caress each other with a growing heat, but he refuses to go quickly. He starts kissing me from my breasts to between my legs, and I'm growing more urgent to have him inside me. At last he enters me and starts a slow, rhythmic motion bringing us both to climax. Lying in his arms, I feel safe and content as I fall asleep.

I awaken with a start. Rob has his hand over my mouth. I struggle to get free, then he motions me to keep quiet and points downstairs. We hear glass shattering and voices. We both quickly dress, and look at each other as we listen to someone, actually more than one, come up the steps.

Rob motions me to get under the bed. I don't hesitate and scoot over to the far side. I put my hand over my mouth so I won't scream. If it's Satchi, disaster can't be far behind. I can hear Rob straightening the covers. Then he walks into the hall and flips on the light.

Satchi yells, "Well, look who we found."

Rob responds, "When did you get back in town?"

Satchi ignores the question and says, "How long you been fucking the ice queen?"

"I'm alone, man. I figure if the broad's not using the house, I might as well make use of it."

"Don't mind if we look around, do you?"

"Knock yourself out."

"I intend to."

I hear sounds of doors opening and slamming shut, and I hear their voices.

"Search in here. I know the bitch is in this house. Where'd you hide her, Rob?"

"I told you, I'm alone."

"I know you've got the hots for the slut. You wouldn't be thinking of double crossing me, now would you?"

"I'm not doing anything. You're the one who left me behind. I thought free room and board sounded too good to pass up."

Suddenly there're more feet coming upstairs.

This time it's Detective Jones. "Okay, drop your guns. You're all under arrest for trespassing."

Thank heavens, it's Jones to the rescue.

"But, Detective, the lady invited us."

"Not a chance, Satchi. Where's Miss Moore?"

I hear Rob say, "She's not here."

"I see. Well, none of you should be either. Okay, officers, get this trash down to the station."

I hear the footsteps of all the men going downstairs. Then someone comes back up and looks under the bed.

Detective Jones asks, "You okay, Miss Moore?"

"Yes, but how did you know I was under here?"

"Rob told me. Talk about a close call. You'd better go back to Indianapolis as soon as possible. I'll delay their releases for as long as I can. All of them were armed, including your buddy."

"Okay, I'll go back." Still under the bed, I wait to be sure everyone is gone before rolling out. Thank heavens the detective arrived when he did. I shudder to think what Rob must be going through locked in a cell with those animals.

Since sleep is out of the question, I finish going through the bedrooms and the bathroom. It's early morning when I finish. I rent an SUV and return to pack up the boxes.

Chapter 15

I arrive back in Indianapolis around two in the afternoon. No one is home, so I leave a message on Gus's phone to let him know I've returned sooner than expected. I also call a realtor in Shipley and explain my plans to her. We agree I'll contact her whenever I get back to town to complete the paperwork to list my home and allow her time to see the property before setting a price.

After I unpack, I go downstairs to prepare dinner and do some light cleaning to make it fresher for everyone. I'm having trouble sitting still as I'm wondering what's going on in Shipley. My phone rings.

"Hi, Rob."

"Hi, Suzanne. Did you get back to Indianapolis okay?"

"Yeah, I'm fine. Are you out of jail?"

"Almost, but Satchi and his group left before me. I wanted to be sure you weren't still in town."

"I left early this morning. Detective Jones said he'd delay their releases to give me a chance to leave, and I didn't have to be told twice. Those guys scare the shit out of me."

"The detective seems like an okay guy."

"I think so, too. Why didn't you get out with the rest of them?"

"The court took us one at time, and I was last. I found out more about what they found in the tunnels."

"Tell me," I prompt.

"They found a satchel with money and some paperwork. They also found a body."

"You mean the skeleton?"

"No, an Amy Johnstone."

This can't be happening. "I thought she was on vacation. I can't believe it."

"They're estimating she's been dead close to six or eight weeks."

I don't know what to say.

"You still there?"

"Yeah. Anything else?"

"Not really. The detective couldn't give me any specific details about the money, paperwork, or identity of the skeleton."

I roll my eyes. "Yeah, the ongoing investigation stuff must be one of his favorite refrains. How was Amy killed?"

"Don't know," Rob responds. "Somehow I bet this all ties together. I'd love to get to the bottom of it, before anyone else gets hurt."

"Yeah, me too."

A little later I hear Gus and Elle return. I go down to see them. They both look sad and tired.

"Gus, how's your aunt?"

"Not well. The doctor said she may not live much longer."

"I'm so sorry."

Gus nods. "Why did you come back early?"

"I ran into Satchi and gang."

"They came back?"

"Yeah, sooner than expected. Luckily I heard them enter my home and was able to hide. Detective Jones arrived before they found me. He carted them off to jail, and he said they all had guns."

"How awful. I shudder to think what might have happened if the detective hadn't shown up. You took quite a chance."

I nod slowly. "True. I have more bad news."

Gus frowns. "What?"

"They found Amy's body in the tunnel by the basement entrance of her store. They estimate she was murdered about eight weeks ago."

Gus sits down, puts his head in his hands, and groans. "Why is all this happening? I don't understand."

"Me either. They also found some cash and paperwork in the satchel we saw."

"Was the money from the bank robbery?"

"Don't know. The detective didn't say."

"Maybe one of these days we'll get some definite answers. I'm beat. We came home to get some rest, and then we'll go back to spend more time with Aunt Ann before Elle leaves tomorrow afternoon to return to Chicago."

"Okay, good night." I watch Gus go up the steps. *He looks like he has the weight of the world on his shoulders.*

***

Sunday passes quietly. On Monday I try to sleep late in preparation for the night shift I start today.

Detective Jones calls around six in the evening. "Miss Moore, I need you and Mr. Breckman to return to Shipley tomorrow. Can you make an 11 a.m. meeting?"

"Yes, I can. I'll let Gus know. He's at the hospital now. His aunt is very ill."

"Tell him this is important. He needs to take the time."

"Are we meeting at your office?"

"No, we'll be in the courthouse in room 124. See you tomorrow."

Before leaving for my job, I call Gus. "How are your aunt and sister doing?"

"Shirley is doing great. My aunt is fading. We're taking it minute by minute."

"Did Elle make her flight?"

"Yeah, she made it back to Chicago safely."

"Good. I have dinner in the crock pot whenever you get home. I'm leaving for the truck stop. I'm going in early tonight to familiarize myself with their routines before I go on duty. I'll return around 8 a.m. By the way, Detective Jones wants to meet with us tomorrow at the courthouse at 11 a.m."

Gus pauses, then says, "What for? Don't you find this unusual?"

"Yeah, I do. And, I thought the detective was a bit stiff."

"I wonder if we're meeting with the prosecutor?"

"He didn't say."

"So what else is new?" Gus sounds weary. "Well, I best get back to my aunt. I hope your job goes okay."

***

I arrive at the truck stop at 9:20 p.m. Even though it's a different type of venue, the basic activities are similar to Gus's Place. By 10:45 p.m. the staff, consisting of a cook and two waitresses, arrive.

"Hi, I'm Suzanne Moore, the new night manager. It's good to meet all of you."

"You're a young one," says Jerry the cook. He's a rough-looking guy in his mid forties. He's almost bald with a ring of close-cropped gray hair. I find out later, this short greeting is one of his longer speeches. He'll usually speak in single syllables, mostly cuss words.

"I'll help you keep these old truckers in line," says Shirley, the older of the two waitresses. She appears a little older than Jerry. She carries herself with a lot of confidence. She's attractive, slim, and has auburn hair tied back in a bun, and makes a clean appearance.

The other waitress, Cathy, appears to be in her early thirties. She's a single mom with a young son. She looks tired, but her uniform is clean.

Shirley explains how the night crowd generally flows. "The truckers are a variety of types and have distinct patterns of when they come and how they eat: one group eats at the end of their drive; the second group, in the middle of their run, are the sandwich and fries guys; and the third group are the early risers trying to get in as many miles as possible before morning rush hour starts. The last group is our breakfast crowd. There are truckers who are nice guys, some are crabs, and a few are lechers. Pretty much typical people. There are more women these days than in the past. Some are by themselves and others are part of a team. Bottom line, we'll keep busy throughout the shift."

"Good to know. I appreciate any help you can give me."

Shirley is right. The night has a steady rhythm with enough time between waves to take care of the housekeeping details. The waitresses handle the customers, and I help Jerry with the orders. I also develop a spreadsheet to keep tabs on the inventory.

As Shirley's getting ready to leave, she says, "Good to have you, Suzanne. I can tell already you'll be a good manager for this place. Welcome!"

"Thanks, Shirley. I'm looking forward to working with everyone."

"Of course you'll like working with Cathy and me, but nobody likes working with Jerry."

Shirley and Cathy walk out together, laughing. Jerry follows behind them, shaking his head.

Yeah, I'm going to like it here.

***

Later that morning, Gus and I arrive at the courthouse. We meet Detective Jones outside Room 124. "Thanks for coming."

Gus says, "What's this all about?"

"Let's go in. We'll explain." The detective opens the door and motions us in. We are formally introduced to Joseph Deekers, the Prosecuting Attorney.

128

Deekers says, "Miss Moore, Mr. Breckman, please have a seat."

For some reason this whole scene is making the hair on my neck tingle.

Detective Jones begins, " We've run into a complication."

I'm confused. "Complication?"

"You were told about a satchel and finding Miss Johnstone's body?"

Together we say, "Yes."

Deekers shifts in his chair. "Can you explain why your fingerprints were found on the case as well as the tool used to kill Miss Johnstone?"

Once again in unison, "What!" I feel faint.

Detective Jones says, "Miss Moore, Mr. Breckman, you lied to me."

"No, we didn't. We never touched the bag. And we never saw Amy," I reply. *This can't be happening.*

Gus sputters, "We didn't. This is impossible."

The detective continues, "What did you do with the contents of the bag?"

Gus says, "What do you mean? I thought you said there was money and paperwork in it."

Jones frowns and shakes his head. "I never told you any such thing. How would you have known the contents if you didn't empty the bag?"

I join in, "Detective, you must have told us. There's no other way we would have known, because we never opened that case."

Mr. Deekers says, "Miss Moore, you seem to know more than the lead detective. The satchel is empty. Neither the detective nor I saw any contents. How else can you explain it?"

"I don't know. Someone told me. We found the skeleton and left immediately. Like I said, we saw the bag but never touched it. We called Detective Jones. That's the last we saw of anything."

Jones says, "Then how did your fingerprints get all over it?"

"We don't know. Suzanne is telling the truth. We didn't touch anything down there." Gus sounds like he's pleading.

Deekers adds, "And how do you explain your fingerprints on the hammer used to kill Miss Johnstone?"

Shaking his head, Gus says, "I can't. It's impossible. I want an attorney. Suzanne and I are done talking. Are we under arrest?"

"Not yet, but don't leave town," says Jones in a more subdued tone.

I suddenly remember my job. "I've got to go back to Indianapolis. I've a job."

Deekers looks up from the paperwork he was looking at and says, "Miss Moore, you have more serious business pending here. Do not leave town."

Gus and I exit the office. As soon as we're on the street, we turn to each other.

I say, "I don't understand. How could this happen?"

"I don't know any more than you do. We need an attorney. We're being framed."

"Satchi?"

"Probably. I'll give my attorney a call now."

While Gus is contacting his lawyer, I call Rob.

"Good to hear from you. What's up? How's the new job?"

"No time to chat. I'm in Shipley. We might be arrested."

"What? Why?"

"For stealing the contents of the bag found next to the skeleton in the tunnel. And worse, we're being accused of killing Amy."

"You told me you never opened the bag."

"We didn't."

"Suzanne, this is crazy."

"Tell me about it. Gus is off the phone. I'll talk to you later."

Gus walks over to me. "We have an appointment at 1 p.m. Let's go get some lunch."

***

Sam Andrews, Gus's lawyer, looks at some papers on his desk while we sit and wait. He sighs, and looks up. "This doesn't look good."

We both shift in our seat. Gus speaks first, "I don't understand how our fingerprints got on the bag. Neither Suzanne nor I touched either the skeleton or the satchel. And, we did not kill Amy."

Andrews asks, "How do you explain your fingerprints getting on those items?"

"I can't. It feels like we're being framed," Gus replies.

I say, "When I was home last weekend, Satchi and his gang broke into my home. They've been in the diner numerous times. Could they have lifted our prints somehow?"

The attorney is silent for a minute. Then he says, "How do I get in touch with Satchi?"

Gus looks like he has a mouthful of something foul. "Beats me. He has a habit of showing up unannounced."

"I see. Miss Moore, how did you know the bag contained both money and paperwork?"

"I was told."

The attorney keeps pressing, "By whom?"

"I thought Detective Jones told me."

Andrews shakes his head. "He denies ever telling you anything about the bag. Could someone else have told you?"

"Maybe." I'm starting to get a sick feeling as I remember Rob's phone call from jail.

"Who else might have told you?" Andrews sounds more demanding now.

Both men are staring at me. *This is not going to go well. But, it's time for complete honesty.* "If the detective didn't tell me, then the only other person I've talked with about any of this would be Rob King."

"Who's Rob?"

Gus nearly spits as he says, "Rob is a member of Satchi's gang. Those guys were extorting money from me and the other shop owners." Gus proceeds to explain to the attorney what's been happening these past few weeks. Neither of them looks pleased.

Andrews looks at me and says, "Let me get this straight. Miss Moore, do you have a relationship with a man who is terrorizing Gus and the other shop owners?"

Before I can respond, Gus yells, "How could you do this, Suzanne? It absolutely disgusts me."

"But, Gus, I--"

The attorney interrupts me. "Are you also in on this extortion, Miss Moore? Are you conning Gus and the other shop owners?"

"NO!"

Andrews continues, "Can you prove it?"

"How can I prove I'm not doing something?"

"Gus, how would you like to proceed?"

Gus asks, "What do you mean?"

"It appears Miss Moore may be involved with a guy who is causing all your troubles. It's not in your best interest for me to provide legal representation for both of you."

I decide to speak up before this goes too far. "I would never betray you, Gus."

"I never thought you could, but I don't know what to think."

The lawyer breaks in. "Gus, I need your decision before we go any further."

"I think Suzanne should get her own attorney."

"No, please don't say that," I beg.

"Miss Moore, I cannot represent you in these matters. Please retain your own attorney and leave my office now."

I start to cry as I look back at Gus. He looks down and won't meet my eyes.

As I stand on the sidewalk outside the courthouse, I feel lost. *What do I do next? I can't lose Gus.*

Chapter 16

I decide to call Legal Aid, and, luckily, they can see me now. I go to their office across the street. Marie Blakely is my appointed attorney. She is in her early thirties, dressed in a white long-sleeved blouse and a navy blue straight skirt. Her dark hair is shoulder length. She's attractive and professional looking. It takes a while for me to explain this whole sordid mess. After I finish, she makes a call to the police.

"Well, Miss Moore..."

"Please call me Suzanne."

She nods. "There's a warrant for your arrest for the murder of Amy Johnstone and the theft of the contents of the satchel found in the tunnel next to the skeleton of Bobby Rawlins."

"But I didn't take anything, and I certainly didn't kill Amy."

Miss Blakely pauses. Then she says, "I believe you, and I'm going to take your case."

I let out the breath I've been holding. "Thank you, Miss Blakely."

"The police are on their way. It's important you talk to no one but me--not to Gus, Rob, Detective Jones, nor Mr. Andrews. Do you understand?"

"Yes, I understand. I need to call my employer and let him know what's going on."

"Do it now."

I call my boss in Indianapolis, who is surprised with my news. As I expected, after only one day on the job, he lets me go. He wishes me luck in getting all this straightened out.

Miss Blakely returns to the room. "Everything okay?"

"Well, I lost my job. But, my boss was nice about it."

"Good. Now to the problem at hand. The police are here for you. I'll come to see you tomorrow with more information about your hearing. Remember, talk to no one about this matter."

"I won't."

I walk out of her office and am handcuffed. I'm read my rights. Then we walk across the street. Talk about your walks of shame. I'm mortified. Once at the station I'm fingerprinted and booked into the jail. It seems like every time I think I've reached bottom, something worse happens.

***

The next morning Detective Jones comes in to interview me.

"Detective, I've been advised by my attorney not to talk with you."

"I understand, but this is important, Miss Moore. How did you find out about the contents of the bag found in the tunnel?"

"I guess this won't hurt. Rob told me. He said you told him about the contents--paperwork and money. He said you couldn't give him any other details."

"Rob told you the truth. Does Gus know about your relationship with Rob?"

I nod. "He didn't when we met with you and the prosecutor, but he does now. He's not speaking to me, and I lost my job. Why didn't you tell the prosecutor you told Rob about the money and paperwork?"

Miss Blakely comes into the room. "Oh good, Suzanne, I see you followed my instructions."

The detective rises and says, "Miss Blakely."

"I want to talk in private with my client."

"Of course. Thank you, Miss Moore."

As soon as the door closes, my attorney starts in on me. "I told you not to talk to anyone. What did you tell him?"

"I wanted him to understand Rob told me about the contents of the bag. And, Rob said Detective Jones told him. The detective confirmed it while he was here today. I wish he would've told the prosecutor. Maybe I wouldn't have been arrested."

"Gus backs you on your version, but he's furious about you and Rob. However, our biggest problem is figuring out how your fingerprints got on the satchel and the hammer."

"We never touched the bag. We did bring a hammer when we explored the tunnel the first day. We left it in the basement. But, that was after Amy had been killed. The fingerprints had to be planted. Such a thing is possible, isn't it?"

"Most experts say it's not possible to do it well."

Can things get any worse? "Super."

"Your prints have been clearly identified as has Gus's. His attorney and I will need to work together. None of this makes sense, and the process won't move as fast as we would like."

"I appreciate your help. I feel lost and haven't any idea how to untangle this mess."

"I'll be back tomorrow when we go before the judge. If you can't make bail, you'll remain in jail until your trial."

I nod. Miss Blakely leaves, and an officer comes in to escort me back to the cell. While I've been away, Gus was brought in. He's in a cell across from mine.

"Gus, are you okay?"

"I'm just peachy. Leave me alone. I've nothing to say to you."

I decide to push for an understanding. "You know I would never betray you. I'm not a part of this gang, but I have gotten close to Rob. He's different. He's trying to help us."

"Yeah right, if he 'helps' any more I'll be spending my retirement in prison. Besides, how do you expect me to believe anything you say? You've let me down."

"I knew you would see my relationship with Rob as a mistake."

"Of course I do. He's playing you."

"He's not playing me, and the truth will come out about him as well as the fact you and I are innocent."

"I'll believe it when I see it."

The jailer comes and tells me I have a visitor. I return to the conference room.

Rob is sitting at the table grinning. "Never thought I'd see you here."

I feel irritated. "Why did you come?"

"Are you okay?"

I look at him in disbelief. "Gus and I are being framed for murder and robbery, Gus is barely talking to me, I lost my job, and I'm in jail. Are you kidding me? Of course, I'm not okay."

Rob drops the smile and leans forward. "Sorry. I'm here to help."

"How?"

"First, answer a few questions. Did you look in the bag when you found it in the tunnel?"

I sigh. "I'm not suppose to talk to anyone but my lawyer. I guess it won't hurt to repeat what I already told you. We never touched or looked in the bag."

"Okay, bear with me. Did you see Amy's body?"

"No. But, there was an awful smell." Closing my eyes I say, " I guess it was her."

Rob gives me a moment to recover. Then he asks, "Who did you call?"

"Detective Jones."

"While you waited for him, did you return to the tunnel?"

"No, we waited upstairs. I've told you this."

Rob is quiet for a minute and then says, "Did you see anyone else go in before the detective arrived?"

"No."

"Who carried the bag outside?"

"I don't know. We left before they came back upstairs. Now let me ask you some questions. Did the detective say there was money and paperwork in the bag?"

Rob pauses. "Yeah, he did. I forgot about our conversation."

"There you go. The contents were intact. We didn't steal anything."

"But it doesn't explain how your prints got there."

"And the circle is complete."

Rob scratches his head. "I'll do my best to find some answers. Do you need anything?"

I shrug as a teardrop falls down my cheek. I get up and go with the guard back to my cell. Gus is gone. Since no one is around, I give in to a long hard cry.

Chapter 17

My attorney shows up to accompany me to court the next morning. I change back to my street clothes. I'm in handcuffs until we reach the courtroom. The procedure goes quickly. The charges are read, and I plead not guilty. My attorney requests bail, and it's set for $50,000. Even though I only have to pay ten percent, it's an amount I can't afford. I'm returned to jail. The pretrial will be held in ten days.

In the afternoon I get a visitor. When I enter the room, Gus is sitting quietly with a stern expression.

Has he decided to forgive me? "It's good to see you!"

"This isn't a social call. I brought back all your things, and I want your permission to put them someplace. Even if you get acquitted, you aren't welcome back to my sister's home."

I lean back in my chair feeling deflated. "You can take the stuff over to my place, but you're overreacting."

"You made your choices, and now I'm making mine. Where can I get a key?"

I'm stunned by his bitterness. For a moment I'm at a loss for words. Seeing no relenting in his eyes, I sigh and say, "There's a spare key hidden in the base of the frog statue in my front garden. It's taped to the inside of the hole. When you are done, lock up and leave the key where you found it."

Gus nods and leaves. I return to my cell. Later in the afternoon, the guard informs me my bail has been posted, and I'm free to go. *Who paid my bail?* As I exit the building, I stop at the bottom of the steps. There's no one waiting for me. *It's terrifying to feel this alone.*

I slowly walk the five blocks to my house. I enter the silence and see the stacks of boxes Gus has brought back. *What happened to our plans? Gus was going to make me a part of his family. What do I have now?*

As I'm slipping into another depressive slump, Rob comes in.

"Thought you might like some gourmet food after the jailhouse slop. I also have a nice bottle of wine." Rob holds up his bags as proof.

"Thanks. Did you pay my bail?"

"Sure, I know you won't flee. I thought you might need some cheering up."

"I do."

"Let's forget all these troubles for tonight."

We eat in silence for a while. I have to admit the food and wine has hit the spot. Then I remember Satchi. "Do I need to be afraid of Satchi showing up?"

"Not tonight. He went back to Columbus with his two tag-a-longs. He thinks you're stuck in jail until your court date."

"Did you ever find out why they go back to Columbus so much?"

"I'm pretty sure they're meeting someone there, but I don't know who. How's Gus?"

"Surly, and he doesn't want me to return to Indianapolis. I knew he'd be upset, but I never dreamed he'd turn on me. It's like he's blaming me for everything." I feel tears welling up.

"Don't give up hope. He does sound like he's made you the scapegoat. He needs time to cool down. Once the truth comes out, he'll change his mind."

"I hope so."

Rob refills our glasses. We drink in silence. I start to think about my future. On Friday I need to check in with my bank about the business loan. What will I do if I get it? Where will I go?

"I don't feel well. I have a bad headache. I think I need some sleep."

"Can I get you anything? How about a massage?"

I shake my head. "How about a rain check? I've some medication I can take. It's just tension. A good night's sleep will help."

"Okay. I'll sleep down here, if it's okay with you."

"Sure. In fact, I like the idea of you being close. Good night."

Thanks to the meds, I fall asleep quickly and sleep soundly all night. I wake up feeling better than I have in a few days. I quickly shower, dress, and go downstairs to find Rob. He greets me with a cup of coffee and a kiss.

"You don't have any food here."

"Sorry, I didn't plan on coming back. Let's go out to eat."

"Together, in public?"

"Why not? Seems like everyone knows about us."

"Still, this might not be the best idea."

"Worried about Satchi or our reputations?"

"Mostly him."

I bring my fist down on the table. "I'm tired of hiding and acting like our relationship is wrong."

Rob holds up his hands in surrender. "You win. Let's go raise some eyebrows."

We settle on a waffle place close to the interstate outside of Shipley but within hiking distance. We linger over breakfast and talk about a whole lot of nothing. For the first time in weeks, I feel relaxed.

Our peace is interrupted. "Well, well, Miss Moore, I see you and Mr. King aren't hiding your relationship."

I sigh. "Detective, we've done nothing wrong."

"To be honest, I hope not."

"I'm afraid of Satchi and his two goons. But Rob has helped me."

"Aren't you taking a chance being seen in public?"

Rob says, "Satchi's out of town."

"Okay, I hope you two know what you're doing."

I turn to Rob and say, "Let's go."

We make the long walk back to my place in silence. *What if I can't prove my innocence?*

Rob gives my hand a squeeze. "Don't let the detective discourage you. Gus is your witness. He may be upset about us, but you know he's an honest man. He won't change his story."

"His anger is so intense. I don't get it."

"We need to get your mind off this crap. What would you like to do today?"

"I guess I'll unpack and go to the grocery store. I'm not feeling very social."

"Why don't you make a list of items, and I'll go to the store. In the meantime, I'll get these boxes to the right rooms."

"Thanks."

He smiles, cups my face with his hand, kisses me gently, and leaves for the front room. After Rob leaves for the grocery, I go upstairs and begin unpacking for my bedroom.

I hear the back door open. At first I think Rob has returned, then I realize there are several people. My heart begins to pound loud enough to be heard. I desperately look around for some type of weapon. It's too late.

Chapter 18

I'm looking at my worst nightmare as I stare at Satchi, Todd, and Luke. I'm speechless.

"Well, the little ice queen is out of jail. Maybe we should celebrate with her. Did you think we wouldn't come back? Nice of lover boy to leave. He'd only spoil our fun." The trio laugh. It's a sickening sound.

My voice returns, "GET OUT."

"Not until I get what I came for. You and Gus owe us money."

"In your dreams. You put Gus out of business."

"So what? You also owe me for legal fees from when you had me arrested."

"I have no money. I can't even get a job because of my legal problems."

"Sucks being you. Use the money you stole."

"I didn't steal anything." *I've got to get out of here. Where's my phone?*

"You're lying. You and Gus split that dough, and now you'll go to prison."

"We're innocent." *I need to buy some time. Please, Rob, hurry back.*

"Everyone in prison says the same thing. But if you're real nice, I'll show you what to expect from your fellow inmates and maybe I'll even let you live to enjoy it...or not." This is followed by more heinous laughter.

Satchi grabs me. I scream as I try to break his hold on my arms. He begins to slug my face. I swing my head from side to side trying to avoid the blows. The pain is intense. He throws me on the bed. I'm fighting him as hard as I can, but now he's straddling me and continuing to hit me. I've never felt so scared and helpless. My arms are held as my blouse and bra are ripped off. I'm trapped. I feel my jeans and panties being dragged off. I can't move. *Please, God, make it stop.* I'm screaming and begging them to leave me alone. I'm losing consciousness. I try to hold on. I can't let these bastards rape me.

***

I must have passed out. I wake up in the hospital. Detective Jones and some woman are standing by the bed.

The woman says, "Miss Moore, can you hear me? I'm Detective Forester. You're in the hospital. You've been badly beaten. Do you understand?"

I barely nod my head. The pain is excruciating.

"Detective Jones is here, too. Miss Moore, the nurse would like to do an examination. She needs your permission. We caught Satchi and his two animals at your place, thanks to Rob. The more evidence we get, the stronger your case."

As I become more awake, I can feel terror growing. I'm finding it hard to breathe and begin clutching my throat. The detectives leave and a nurse comes in. She explains what she'll be doing and why. I agree to the procedure. She works quietly and gently. She explains she has been able to collect some semen and hair. She is able to get some skin from beneath my nails.

The nurse says, "The worst injuries are to your head and face. You have a concussion, your nose is broken, and you have several skin abrasions on your face. We are going to put stitches on the cut above your left eye. Your vagina is torn and will also need a few stitches. We want to keep you here for twenty-four hours to be sure there are no complications. You're safe here, and you're close to the nurse's station."

I shudder and start to cry.

She gently pats my hand. "I know it doesn't seem like it, but you will survive this."

"I don't think I can," I sob.

After tending to my wounds, the nurse says, "I know this is a bad time, but those detectives are waiting to see you. Do you feel okay to talk?"

"Yes." *Let's get it over with.*

The two detectives come back in. Jones says, "Miss Moore, thank you for seeing us. We'll keep it short as we know you're in a lot of pain."

I gingerly nod.

"Can you tell us what happened?"

I explain Rob leaving for the store and the arrival of the three guys while I was upstairs and alone. I'm interrupted as Detective Jones has me list the three names. Then I tell them about the beating and my clothes being torn off, but it's all I can remember. By the time I finish, I'm sobbing.

"Who was hitting you?"

I gasp, "Satchi."

"When did Rob come back in?"

"I never saw him."

Detective Forester is writing in a notebook. "Thank you, Miss Moore. I'm so sorry this happened to you. We have everything we need to make the charges stick. We'll do our best to ensure they don't get out soon."

"Thank God."

"Do you have any questions?"

"No."

"Try to get some rest. You've been through an awful ordeal."

After the detectives leave, the nurse returns. "How are you doing?"

"It feels like my head is swollen, my nose hurts, and I feel like my body has been ripped in half. Is there any chance I'll get pregnant? I'm on birth control pills, but I can't remember when I last took one."

"The doctor has prescribed pain medication and a morning-after pill, if you want it. It will take time for all the swelling to go down everywhere."

"I want the pill. There's no way I'd carry that monster's baby."

After I take the medication, she says it's okay to sleep and she'll be back to check on me. She places the buzzer in my hand.

After she leaves, Rob comes in. "How are you?"

"Awful. You look like you got a beating, too."

"Those guys look much worse. When I got back from the store, I saw the back door was kicked in. I knew you were in trouble. I called

149

9-1-1 immediately. As I ran into the house, I heard the commotion upstairs. I wanted to kill Satchi once I saw what he was doing to you. The police were there in no time and got all of them. The ambulance was right there, too. They whisked you away before I could get back to you. I'm so sorry. I should never have left you alone."

"Did you know they were coming?"

"Of course not. Why would you say that?"

"It seems like you leave and Satchi shows up. It's happened before."

"I would never hurt or betray you. Please, believe me."

"I want to."

"Do you want me to go?"

I pause. "No, please don't leave me alone. The nurse said I can sleep, and I think she gave me something to help. I have to stay here overnight."

"Of course I'll stay. I'm so sorry. It must've been awful."

"It was." I start to cry again.

Rob tries to keep me occupied until I fall asleep. The same nurse, as well as a couple other staff, come in on a regular basis to check my vitals. I find it difficult to even sip water.

In the morning, a social worker comes in to talk. She is kind and supportive. She emphasizes contacting a trauma counselor once I return home. She gives me a card with a therapist's information. The doctor comes in around noon and tells me I can go home, if I promise to take it easy. They say I need to have someone with me. Rob is there and says he won't leave me alone. They don't blink an eye and accept his assistance as usual fare. They warn me to keep the facial stitches dry for a week. They wish me well and leave.

I shoo Rob out and put on the outfit he brought me from home. When I open the door to leave, Rob is waiting right there. He puts his arms around me and gently holds me for a minute. I stand stiffly until he lets go. As soon as I get home, I shower, taking care to keep my stitches dry, and scrub my skin raw until the hot water runs out. I wonder if I'll ever feel clean, and I wonder if I'll ever be able to let another man touch me intimately.

Rob meets me when I come out of the bathroom. "I set you up in the other bedroom. I've cleaned up as best I could. The police were here while you were gone. They took the bed coverings and dusted for prints everywhere. I boarded up the back door for tonight. I'll fix it properly in the morning."

"Thanks."

"Are you hungry."

"No."

"Well, let me know if you change your mind. I'll be in the other bedroom."

I nod and shut the door of my new bedroom. There's an old recliner in this room. I flip up the foot rest and reach for the glass of wine Rob has poured for me. Lying in bed doesn't appeal to me tonight. I wish Rob had left me the whole bottle.

I sleep restlessly all night. Every time I doze off, I relive the whole nightmare. Pictures of Satchi's sneering face and being constantly hit make me wake up screaming a couple times. At some point during the night, I must have grabbed a blanket. In the morning I find I'm covered. As I wake up more, I see Rob asleep on the bed. I have to admit, it's a comforting sight. I feel awful.

151

Rob sits up and stretches. "Good morning. How're you doing? You were having nightmares."

"I guess my screaming gave me away."

"I wish I could ease your pain."

"Can you keep my life from getting any worse?"

"I hope so. Satchi won't be getting out on bail this time." He straightens the covers. Slowly he sits down on the bed next to my chair.

"I hate this happened to you. I hate Satchi, and I never wanted to come between you and Gus."

I can't respond because I'm crying again. I shake off his attempt to hug me and leave to go to the bathroom. I startle when I catch sight of myself in the mirror, nothing is better. My face is swollen with half a variety of different colors where there aren't bandages. *My face matches my mood.*

I freshen up and put on a clean blouse and jeans. I go downstairs and find Rob in the kitchen.

"How about something to eat?"

"Thanks, but I only want juice and coffee."

"Sit down and I'll bring them to you. Hope you don't mind, I made some pancakes. Sure you don't want something like toast or bacon and eggs?"

"No, go ahead and eat. I'm not hungry."

My phone rings. "Hello?"

"Suzanne, this is Marie Blakely. I talked with Detective Forester. Are you okay? Of course you're not. I'm on my way over."

Putting the phone down, I say, "My attorney is coming here."

"Probably wants to help you prosecute Satchi and his gang."

"If I haven't thanked you for staying with me last night, thank you. I appreciate your support." This sounds as flat as I feel.

"You don't need to thank me. I was out of my mind with fear when I saw the back door kicked in. I feel so guilty not being there for you."

"You know, it's strange."

"What?"

"Does anyone, besides me, know you're a private investigator?"

Rob shakes his head. "I don't think so."

"I'm surprised the police didn't arrest you, too."

"When I called for help, I gave my name. When they arrived, I was fighting those three guys so they couldn't leave."

"I guess you can't rejoin them. Do you care?"

"Not for the reason you might think."

"What do you mean?"

Chapter 19

The doorbell rings before Rob can answer. I let my lawyer in and take her into the living room.

Miss Blakely says, "You poor thing, your face. I heard you had a concussion. Should you be up?"

"The doctor said I'm okay and gave me some pain pills."

"I know you were savagely beaten. I'm so sorry. The good news is the hospital was able to collect a significant amount of evidence against Satchi. The judge denied bail for all three of them due to the violence of the attack."

"What a relief."

"Do you need anything?"

"I'm okay. Rob is helping me. I feel nervous and on the verge of hysteria."

After Rob finishes cleaning up the kitchen, he enters the room. "Any news about her court case?"

Marie says, "Is it okay with you if he's here?"

"It's fine. Rob knows everything I know."

Rob says, "I'm wondering if the contents of the satchel are at the bottom of all this."

"You mean the money?" I ask.

"Not so much. I think the paperwork might be more pertinent. Maybe it's a deed or a will."

I ask, "Miss Blakely, can you find out about the paperwork?"

She looks puzzled. "I'm confused. The forensic department's report said the bag was empty."

Rob shakes his head. "Detective Jones told me there was money and paperwork. He didn't give me any details due to it being an ongoing investigation."

"He told you directly?"

"Yes, he told me when I was in jail last week or whenever it was."

"Will you testify in court to that?"

"Yes."

I say, "Now *I'm* confused. Do you think Detective Jones has been lying to me? This is troubling."

Miss Blakely says, "Good question. I need to talk with him. Do you have any questions about the charges against the men who attacked you?"

"Will I have to testify?"

"Yes, I'm afraid so. I doubt Satchi will plead guilty out of the goodness of his heart."

I begin to cry. Miss Blakely tries to soothe me with calming words. My tears finally end, and Miss Blakely gets ready to go. We agree to talk more later, and Miss Blakely leaves.

Rob says, "Maybe she'll be able to find some answers for us."

With a sigh, I say, "I hope she doesn't get killed."

I go up to my substitute bedroom. I take some pain medication, lie down, and stare at the ceiling. As I start to drift off, I hear a soft knock on the door.

Rob sticks his head in. "I'm going out for a while. No one should bother you. I'll bring us some lunch. If you get hungry before then, there's cold cuts in the refrigerator."

"Okay."

"I've fixed the back door. Everything is locked up tightly. Do you need anything while I'm out?"

"No." I turn away from him. I know I won't sleep if he leaves. It's better anyway, since I'm afraid to sleep and have the nightmares come back.

***

A little later, I hear the doorbell. I drag myself downstairs to see who it is. Through the glass I see Detectives Jones and Forester are standing there.

Jones says, "May we come in? How are you doing, Miss Moore?"

"Okay. What's up?"

"Are you alone?"

"Yes, Rob said he'd be back around lunch time."

"Good, we need to talk with you in private."

They look so serious, I know it's bad news. "You're scaring me."

"Satchi escaped from our jail sometime after midnight."

I begin to tremble and feel faint. "This can't be happening."

Jones says, "We want to put you into protective custody."

"What does that mean?" I back up to a chair and sink into it.

"We have a safe house you can stay in."

Then Detective Forester says, "We believe Satchi will come after you."

I say, "He's obviously getting all kinds of help. Where can I go to be safe?" I want to scream.

She continues, "I can only imagine how you're feeling. We're thinking the same thing about possible contacts. We're taking you to the safe house ourselves. We'll give you a burner phone for emergencies, as you'll be leaving your phone here. Only four people know of this arrangement besides us. We handpicked them, so there are no leaks or hidden agendas going on."

Detective Jones says, "Rob cannot know where you are. We can't guarantee your safety if anyone else knows your whereabouts."

"When do we go?"

"Now. Detective Forester will help you pack. I'll keep watch down here."

I'm glad for the detective's company. I don't want to be alone in the bedroom where I was attacked. "For how many days am I packing?"

"One week will work. There's a washer and dryer on the premises."

I quickly pack my clothes and toiletries. We go back downstairs where Detective Jones is watching the street.

"Give me a couple minutes after I leave, then you two meet me in the alley."

"Can I leave a note for Rob telling him I'm safe?"

Jones says, "No. You may trust him, but we don't."

Detective Forester and I wait as instructed. We hurry as fast as I can walk with my injuries out to the alley. I notice her hand is on her revolver. When Detective Jones pulls up, we jump into the car.

"Did you see anything, Jones?"

"No."

Their terse speech is doing nothing for my frayed nerves. I have no idea where we are going, and the detectives tell me it's better that way. We drive around for a while before we pull into a garage. The door goes down, and we exit to the attached house. I'm estimating the building to be about twenty years old. It's clean and decorated minimally. We enter through the kitchen where we find two men sitting at the table. Detective Forester introduces me to Officers John Cleary and Tom Hald. They explain I'll have two officers with me at all times. I'm shown my room and unpack my belongings. Attached to my room is a full bathroom. After settling in, I rejoin the four officers.

Detective Jones says, "Miss Moore--"

"Please call me Suzanne."

"Okay, Suzanne, it's vital you don't let anyone know where you are. Under no circumstances are you to call Rob, Gus, or even your attorney. The phone is only for emergencies."

"I promise. But, won't Rob and Miss Blakely be concerned about my whereabouts?"

"We'll handle contacting your attorney and Rob. Keep the phone with you at all times. Two more officers, Bates and Miles, will come at nine tonight and stay until Cleary and Hald return at seven tomorrow morning. All the officers know one another, and there will be no substitutes. Their job is to keep you safe. Any questions?"

"I get it, and I appreciate all of you. I hope you catch Satchi soon."

The detectives leave, and I turn to face the two remaining officers.

Tom Cleary stands about 5'9" and looks to be about thirty-five. John Hald is slightly taller and appears to be the same age. Both officers are dressed casually in jeans. Both are armed and wear badges on chains around their necks.

Officer Cleary smiles and says, "Try to relax. Feel free to watch television, get a snack, read, sleep or do whatever, but stay inside and away from the windows. We'll be here roaming around, keeping an eye on things. Supper is at six."

"Okay. Thanks for being so nice. I appreciate it. But to tell you the truth, I want to be alone. I'll be in my room."

At some point I must have fallen asleep. The next thing I know I'm screaming, and Officer Hald is gently shaking my arm.

"Wake up, Suzanne. It's okay. You're safe. You're having a bad dream. Dinner's ready."

I nod as I wake up. "Okay, I'll be out shortly."

Hald leaves, and I lie back down. I realize I've got to eat something. I get up, wash my face gently, and then go out to the kitchen.

Cleary sets a bowl of soup and a salad in front of me. "Here are some crackers. I'm not a gourmet cook, but I know how to open cans. We have a simple, but adequate, food supply. What would you like to drink? We have many choices including water, iced tea, soft drinks, wine and beer."

"A glass of iced tea sounds good. Thanks."

"Hald will be in shortly. He's walking the perimeter. We carry radios to keep track of each other."

"Do you have to use this safe house often?"

"No, but when we do, we follow a strict routine for the safety of everyone, as the detective explained."

"Are you familiar with this group terrorizing us?"

"I've seen them at the station. Satchi's a real head case and needs to be put away."

I softly say, "The whole thing's a nightmare: the extortion, the beatings, the fires, and the deaths of Jessica and Amy."

Cleary says, "I hear you. Jessica was a friend of mine. I want her killer punished."

Officer Hald enters the room. "Sounds like you two are having a serious discussion."

"We're sharing our frustrations over not being able to solve these crimes and bring the guilty to justice," replies Cleary.

"Yeah, " Hald joins us at the table. "Obviously something isn't right."

I say, "I don't understand why Jessica or Amy were murdered. What did they know? And how did our fingerprints get on everything? We never touched the bag, and we never killed Amy."

Hald says, "Have you heard from Breckman?"

"Gus is upset with my being with Rob. I've nothing against Gus, but now he thinks he can't trust me. This really hurts."

Cleary says, "Your boyfriend is part of the gang. Why wouldn't Gus be suspicious?"

I gasp. "I'm not part of the group. Rob is different. He's good to me."

Cleary stops washing dishes and turns to me. "It sounds dangerous. How can you be sure Rob isn't playing you?"

I stare at Cleary. *Here we go again. How do I explain when I've promised not to tell?*

"I can see from your facial expression, you understand where I'm coming from."

"I understand, but my instincts say he's okay. Rob called the police when Satchi attacked me, and I was told he fought all three guys to help me." I accept a second glass of iced tea and return to my room. I flip on television and spend the next couple of hours watching reruns of sitcoms.

***

At shift change, all four of my guards troop into my room. Officer Hald does the introductions and tells me he and Cleary will be back early tomorrow. The three men leave, Officer Karen Bates remains. I estimate she is about 5'7" tall. She's around 30 and has short dark hair.

"I heard what happened to you. I'm sorry." She's silent for a moment, then softly says, "I'm a survivor. I'm here to listen if you want to talk. I know I'm a stranger, but sometimes it's easier to talk to a person you don't know."

I've no idea when I started to cry, but I'm soon sobbing. Bates makes an attempt to put her arm around me, but I lean back to avoid her touch. She nods at my action and doesn't say a word. As I quiet down, she hands me some tissues.

"Thanks, Officer. It feels good to cry. I guess I'm all feelings with no words."

"It's okay. The words will come. I need to go check with my partner. If you need me or if you would like some company, come on out. We won't be sleeping."

Alone again, I lean back on the headboard. I feel calmer but troubled at the same time. I think of Gus and hope he and his sister are safe. I miss him and wonder if he'll ever forgive me.

About an hour later there's a knock on the door. Officer Bates enters and turns out my light. "There's someone on the premises. Come with me."

Chapter 20

I follow her into the hall where Miles joins us. I'm now sandwiched between them, and they have their guns drawn. I think I have forgotten how to breathe. We listen.

Then Miles whispers, "Roger that. Back up is on the way."

Bates quietly says in my ear, "Someone is outside. Help is on the way. We stay here. If someone enters, I'll confront them, and you'll go with Officer Miles. Understand?"

I nod. We stand in silence for what seems like forever. Suddenly there are crashing sounds at the back door. Bates makes her way out of the hall and turns toward the kitchen. Miles pulls me into another bedroom, closes the door, and tells me to go out the window if our uninvited guest starts to come in. He tells me to jump out, turn right, and go to the next block, where I'll find a dark blue Chevy SUV. I'm to get in, lock the door, and lie down on the floor until help arrives. He tells me how the officers will identify themselves.

I silently pray none of this will be necessary, as I'm sure it would mean the two officers are dead. I begin to tremble and feel faint. I will myself not to have a panic attack. Not now. I have to do my part.

Bang--bang--bang. We hear shots being fired and a lot of yelling. Miles positions himself to the side of the door with his gun raised. We hear two quick knocks, a pause, then three quick knocks.

Bates says, "All clear, Miles."

He unlocks the door and slowly opens it. His gun is still out. He puts it back in a holster when he sees Bates is alone.

Miles motions me to come out to the hall.

I ask, "What happened?"

"The detectives shot the guy. He has no ID. Jones and Forester are taking him to the station after they get him patched up."

I'm shivering as I say, "How the hell did he find the safe house?"

Bates says, "That's a question I'd like answered, too."

"So a gunman was sent to keep me from testifying against Satchi?"

"Most likely."

Although no one says it, my guess is there's a mole in the police department. Neiher officer looks happy, so I assume they might be thinking the same thing.

Officer Bates returns. "We're going to move you to another safe house."

"You really think there's any use?"

She shrugs and points to my room.

I sigh and say, "I'll pack my things."

The two officers and I climb into a sedan with darkened windows. We drive about half an hour. Neither one has much to say. We arrive at another modest brick home. Bates drives the car into the attached garage. The door is closed before we exit into the house. Milcs docs a quick run through.

When he returns, he says, "All clear in here. I'll go outside and check the perimeter."

Bates responds, "Good. Come on, Suzanne, I'll show you your room."

Once she does, Bates asks, "Do you need anything?"

"No, I'm fine. It's time to take my pain meds, and I'll probably take a nap."

"Good, you need your rest."

Despite my racing mind, I can't fight my fatigue and quickly fall asleep. The next thing I know it's morning. My watch says 7:45. I can hear people talking. I freshen up and join them in the kitchen.

Bates says, "Good morning, Suzanne. Would you like some coffee?"

"Sounds great. Good morning, Officers. Where's Miles?"

Hald says, "He's out checking around the house."

"Any updates on the guy from last night?"

Cleary says, "Not yet."

"This is bizarre. I'm being hunted by unknown people for unknown reasons."

Cleary says, "By the way, Detective Jones gave me this letter for you."

"Thanks, I'll take it and my coffee to my room.

The letter is from Rob:

Dear Suzanne,

I became worried when I returned the other day and you were gone. I went to the police station to see Jones. He told me you were safe. He also told me Satchi had escaped. Please be careful. I wish I could be with you, but I know you can't contact me. I understand. Be safe,   Rob

***

The next several days are quiet. I'm taken to see my attorney the day before my court date.

Miss Blakely asks, "Are you okay?"

"Sort of. My wounds seem to be slowly healing."

"Good. I hope you're getting some rest after your trauma."

"Yeah, I guess you can call it rest. What's going to happen tomorrow?"

"We're having a pretrial where the judge will review the evidence. There won't be a jury at this proceeding. I can't explain the fingerprints, but a thorough search of your house, Gus's apartment, and the diner turned up nothing. We have to see how the prosecutor plays the prints."

I nod my understanding, and say, "Did you find out what was in the paperwork?"

"It's been difficult. There might have been several account summaries, some deeds, and a will."

"Deeds? A will? Can you tell me more about any of it?"

166

Miss Blakely shows a pained expression "Sorry, no. This information was based on reports from the original bank robbery."

"So, where are the documents?"

She shrugs and says, "No one seems to know. I have a well-respected fingerprint expert scheduled to testify. I believe he will raise reasonable doubts."

"Will I testify?"

"Not at this procedure, but you will if we go to trial."

I feel disappointed by her statement, but I trust she knows what she's doing.

Officer Hald arrives to escort me back to the safe house. Miss Blakely has gotten several outfits for me to wear tomorrow and for however long a trial might last. Hald helps me carry these things to the car.

On the way, I ask him if Satchi has been caught or if the shooter was identified.

"No to both questions. We're checking ballistics to see if this gun was used in Jessica's death."

***

The next morning, Officer Bates accompanies me to the courthouse. She sits with me until Miss Blakely arrives. The Judge enters and the pretrial begins.

The attorneys give their opening statements describing their cases. Mr. Deekers mentions no eyewitnesses, no motive, only the fingerprints. He begins by calling an Officer Baldwin, who testifies about the processing of these prints. He verifies the report is the one he wrote.

I want to jump up and shout "Liar,liar," but I've been warned to keep quiet no matter what is said.

Next the prosecutor calls a professional fingerprint expert to the stand. This guy testifies fingerprints of such clarity can't be planted.

Then Detective Jones is on the stand. He answers questions about the day the skeleton was found and finishes with my arrest at the Legal Aid office. He denies seeing the contents of the bag. No mention is made of all the trouble at Gus's Place and the other shops. The way the prosecutor is setting it up, I could be a first-class liar and thief.

I'm impressed with how Miss Blakely cross examines everyone. She does get the detective to mention Gus and all the trouble with Satchi. I think she is very convincing.

The judge adjourns court until after lunch.

Miss Blakely says, "I'm having our lunch brought to the interview room. We'll have a guard."

"Do we need one to protect us from Satchi?"

"Yes, but the risk is low. Please don't worry. Have you talked with Rob?"

"No, I haven't talked with him since I was put in the safe house."

"The guy is a mystery. I haven't figured out his angle yet."

"You mean I don't seem like the type to warrant such devotion?"

She rolls her eyes. "Get real. A whirlwind romance starting at the same time as this trouble?"

I feel hurt by her words, but I can't defend him without revealing his undercover work.

After lunch it's Miss Blakely's turn to lay out our argument. Her first witness is Gus. She asks him to describe our exploration of the tunnel. He testifies we went into the tunnel after surmising there might be something on the premises causing the interest in these properties. He describes cutting through the openings, and then he tells about the skeleton and the bag we found. He goes on to say he stopped me from touching the bag, and he tells about the horrible odor. He relates how we left and called Detective Jones, and he emphasizes we waited upstairs and never saw the bag or knew what was causing the smell.

Miss Blakely asks Gus to tell the court how he feels about my associating with Rob. He says I hid it from him. She asks him why he is testifying on my behalf if he is so upset with me. Gus replies he's only telling the truth.

Once it's his turn, the prosecutor makes the point Gus is facing the same charges as I am. Gus acknowledges it.

Miss Blakely redirects by asking, "Gus, have you been offered any deals to testify at this proceeding?"

Gus says, "No."

The judge announces we are recessed until tomorrow morning.

"How do you think it's going, Miss Blakely?"

"I'll be honest. Gus's testimony was strong, but your relationship with Rob is damaging your case."

"Will Rob testify?"

"If I can find him."

"What do you mean? He sent me a letter through Detective Jones. He sounded like he wanted to help."

"Do you have it with you?"

"Yes, here." I pull the letter from my pocket.

"Detective Jones gave you this letter?"

"No, Officer Cleary gave it to me, but he said he got it from the detective."

Miss Blakely motions to Cleary. He comes over and confirms what I said.

Miss Blakely frowns. She says, "Rob is nowhere to be found. Without his testimony, we can't throw doubt on the chain of custody of the weapon and the bag. We'll go to trial."

I'm speechless. *Is everyone right about Rob?*

Chapter 21

We return to the courthouse in the morning. I cried on and off most of the night. I'm scared, and I must look like a sorry creature with my blotchy skin, healing facial wounds, and bloodshot eyes.

"Did you find Rob?" My heart sinks, as I realize the answer by Miss Blakely's sad expression.

"No. I'm so sorry, and I'm out of ideas of where to look."

Court begins. The judge asks Miss Blakely if she has any other witnesses. She looks at me before she answers. "Your honor, we have another witness, but--"

She is interrupted by a commotion at the back of the room. The door is pushed open, and Rob bolts in. I'm so relieved to see him, I stand and turn towards him.

The judge is banging his gavel for order. "Sit down, Miss Moore."

Miss Blakely says, "Your honor, I see my next witness has arrived. I call Robert King to the stand."

Rob comes to the front and is sworn in. Miss Blakely begins her questioning.

"Please state your name and address for the court."

"My work name is Rob King, and my legal name is Robert Clinger. I reside at The National Motel on 101 Brown Street, Room C, in Shipley."

"Is this your permanent address?"

"No, it's temporary. I live in Kingston."

"What is your occupation, Mr. King?"

"I'm a private investigator."

"What is your business here in Shipley?"

Rob responds, "I was hired to find a killer."

"Hired by whom?"

"The family's name is Hoskins."

"Can you explain the nature of your investigation?"

"They hired me to find the men responsible for their son's death."

Miss Blakely seems surprised with his response. She stops moving, turns to him, and asks, "Isn't that a police matter?"

"Yes, it is. However, the police haven't had any leads for six months. The family was desperate for answers."

"Are you a member of Satchi's gang?"

"I was working undercover, but I'm not anymore."

"Why did you join this group?"

"My investigation pointed to these three guys. So I joined them to get more evidence."

"Has Miss Moore been helping you with this investigation?"

"No. I didn't hire her nor did my clients."

"Why did you begin a relationship with Miss Moore?"

Rob glances at me before he answers. "At first, the flirtation was part of my act and my clumsy attempt to protect her. As I got to know her, I began to care for her." As he answers, I want to die of embarrassment.

Miss Blakely continues. "In the middle of an undercover job?"

Rob shifts in his seat. "I know it wasn't the smartest thing."

"When did you find out about the bag found with the skeleton of Bobby Rawlins?"

"Suzanne told me she and Gus saw it in the tunnel under the diner."

"Did she tell you what it contained?"

"No. She told me they didn't look inside."

"Did you speak about this bag to anyone else?"

"Yes, I spoke with Detective Jones."

"Where and when did this conversation take place?"

"I'd been arrested for trespassing a couple days after the bag was found. The detective told me while I was in jail."

Miss Blakely glances at her notes. "What did the detective tell you about the contents?"

"He told me there was money and paperwork in it."

The prosecutor interrupts. "Objection. The detective has already testified to his findings."

"Overruled. I'll allow it."

"Thank you, your Honor. How much money and what kind of paperwork?"

"He wouldn't say because it was part of an ongoing investigation."

"I have no more questions at this time." Miss Blakely returns to our table.

The prosecutor puts down his pen, gets up, and slowly walks toward Rob. "Do you have a private investigator's license, Mr. King?"

"Yes, it's in my back pocket." Rob pulls a holder out of his pocket, flips it open to show a badge and an identification card, and hands it to the prosecutor. The bailiff takes the license and badge, gets them logged in, and hands it to the judge.

"Why didn't you tell Miss Moore about your undercover work?"

"At first, I didn't know her well. Once I started to have feelings for her, I did tell her what I was doing. I asked her to keep it confidential. I didn't want to blow my cover, for our mutual safety."

"Was anyone else aware of your work as a private investigator?"

"Only the family I mentioned before."

"I see. Why would Detective Jones tell you about the contents of the bag or anything found in the tunnel?"

"I don't know. Maybe he was trying to see what I knew."

Mr. Deekers looks at the judge as he says, "Or maybe the conversation never took place and you're covering for someone else."

Miss Blakely rises and says, "Objection, your Honor. Prosecution is badgering the witness."

"Sustained."

"I have no more questions for this witness."

"Do you have any other witnesses, Miss Blakely?"

"Yes, your honor. I would like to recall Detective Jones to the stand."

"Very well. We are in recess until this afternoon." He bangs his gavel and exits.

Miss Blakely turns to me once the judge leaves. "So you knew Rob is a private investigator?"

"Yes, but he asked me not to tell anyone. Is the fact he's a P.I. good or bad news?"

"I'm not sure. Still sounds like you were being played."

"I don't think so. He didn't have to testify. It made him blow his cover.

"You're hopeless. Officer Cleary will take you to the interview room for lunch."

***

I don't see Miss Blakely again until we go back to the courtroom after the recess. Rob is nowhere in sight. Miss Blakely recalls Detective Jones to the stand.

"Detective, were you present during Robert King's testimony this morning?"

"No."

"You testified earlier you did not see the contents of the bag. Did you tell Mr. King there was money and papers in it?"

"I was told by a member of the forensics team there was money and other stuff. When I received a copy of the report, it said the bag was empty."

"How do you explain the discrepancy?"

"I can't."

"Is it possible Miss Moore did not take the contents."

Prosecutor says, "Objection, your Honor. Calls for speculation."

"Overruled. I'll allow it."

"Would you like me to repeat the question, Detective Jones?"

"No. It's possible Miss Moore did not take anything from the bag. I don't know who did what."

"Thank you, Detective."

The judge asks the prosecutor if he has any questions. The prosecutor responds he does and approaches Detective Jones.

"Are you now testifying a member of the forensics team is responsible for the theft?"

"I'm saying I received two different reports."

"Who reported there were contents in the bag?"

"Jason Baldwin told me on the phone the same day the bag and weapon were found."

The prosecutor hands a sheet to the detective. "Is this the report you saw later?"

"Looks like it." Jones hands the sheet back.

After the prosecutor hands the report to the bailiff, he continues, "Who signed the written report?"

"Jason Baldwin."

"Are you claiming Mr. Baldwin lied to you?"

"I don't know what happened. I was told one thing and the report said another."

"No more questions for this witness."

The judge says, "You are dismissed, Detective Jones." Then he calls for closing arguments.

Mr. Deekers goes first. He emphasizes my fingerprints found on the hammer used to kill Amy Johnstone and on the case. He goes on to tell the judge my motive was greed. He states I took the money and killed Amy Johnstone when she tried to stop me. He says I played both Gus and Rob to hide my guilt.

Miss Blakely argues my case from the view of innocent victim. The hammer found by Amy Johnstone's body had been moved from the diner where Gus and I first attempted to open the blocked wall after Miss Johnstone died. She argues the fingerprints on the case were either planted or fabricated, since there is a question of the two different reports. She points to the forensics department for losing evidence. She denies any evidence of a motive for my doing either crime.

They both gave good closing arguments. I hope the judge sees the validity of Miss Blakely's.

At 2:30 the judge leaves telling us he will give us his decision tomorrow morning. There's nothing to do but return to the safe house.

Before leaving, Miss Blakely says, "Gus's and Rob's testimonies were convincing. The detective was a big help, too. Hopefully they convinced the judge the prosecutor has no case."

"Is Gus in a safe house?" I ask.

"Yes, Detective Jones is taking no chances. He wants all the charges against Satchi and those other guys to stick. He'd really like to get the kingpin's name."

"Wouldn't we all."

Chapter 22

Rising the next day I feel refreshed until I think of Rob. I tell myself I don't need Rob. He has a job to do, and I'm no longer a part of the assignment. I care for him, but maybe our timing is wrong. I shower, dress, and go out to the kitchen. My two day officers are at the table drinking coffee.

"Good morning."

Cleary smiles and shakes his head. "Rob's a good undercover agent. He fooled a lot of us." He sets a plate of scrambled eggs, bacon and toast in front of me.

I respond, "I think it's great he's helping that family find their son's killer. I'm relieved everyone knows he's a P.I."

Hald joins us at the table. "I wonder how he found Satchi?"

I shrug. "I don't know. Unfortunately, his cover is completely blown, and the whole situation is making me sad."

Hald nods and says, "If he hadn't testified and identified his line of work, he could still be pursuing his lead. He sabotaged his own progress by appearing in court on your behalf."

I raise my eyebrows, and ask, "Are you trying to make me feel guilty?"

Hald smiles and shakes his head. "Not at all. He put you ahead of his work. That's saying something."

Cleary hands me a cup of coffee. "He did take you into his confidence once he got to know you. He probably won't get paid until he comes back with the evidence."

"Well, I hope he's able to get a ton of evidence against Satchi." I finish my breakfast.

Both officers reply in unison, "Amen."

Cleary stands. "Ready to go?"

I nod and say to Hald, "Keep your fingers crossed."

"You got it." He closes the door behind us.

As we drive to the courthouse, I ask, "Has the intruder been identified?"

"Not yet. Sometimes the system is slow."

I nod. "Do we think Satchi, Todd, Luke, and the John Doe are all working for the same guy?"

"Probably."

"Could Reis be the leader?"

"We've no proof. We need one of these guys to talk."

"I always thought Jessica got killed because she found out something about why Reis is so anxious to get those properties."

Cleary doesn't respond and turns his attention to watching the road and the rearview mirror.

I start watching the side mirror. Then I remember. "Has her photographer come back to town? Has anyone spoken with him?"

Cleary asks, "Who?"

"John Burton, Jessica's photographer. He disappeared right after her murder."

"No one has seen him. He's probably in hiding, thinking he could be next."

"I wish we knew what she had discovered. I know she was going to Columbus the next day to talk with a lobbyist. Columbus seems to be a popular city."

Cleary asks, "What do you mean?"

"Satchi and gang went there a couple times since I've known them. Rob told me those guys are from there as is Reis."

"Could be a coincidence." Cleary's quiet for a few minutes. Then he says, "I think Jessica was seeing someone in Columbus."

"Who?"

"She never told me his name. I thought he might be married."

We're quiet for the rest of our trip.

As we get out of the car, I say, "I'd like to talk with the photographer. Does anyone know how to reach him?"

"Even if we did, you can't contact anyone."

"This is frustrating. Who knows how many gunmen may be out there."

"We want to know how the first one found you."

"A mole in the police department?"

"Looking like it."

"But why? Money?"

"Greed, revenge, jealousy--these are some of the usual motives."

"I wonder if any of them fit our current situation?"

We enter the courtroom at five minutes to nine. The lawyers are present and at their tables. We join Miss Blakely, and she nods to us. The judge enters. We retake our seats.

The judge begins, "I'll get straight to the point. The issue of the fingerprints on the murder weapon and the satchel is inadmissible due to improper chain of custody. Further, I rule there is insufficient evidence to proceed to trial. Miss Moore, you are free to go without prejudice. Mr. Deekers, if you will join me in chambers." He bangs his gavel and leaves.

I'm in shock and say, "That's it? It's over?"

Miss Blakely turns to me with a big smile. "Yes, it's over. You are free to go." She hugs me.

I look over at the prosecutor who appears angry as he tosses a file into his briefcase and hurries out behind the judge. I wonder if the mole is in the forensics department. But it's not my problem. I'm free.

Officer Cleary comes up and lightly touches my shoulder. "Congratulations, Suzanne. I hate to spoil the moment, but we need to leave now."

"Thank you again, Miss Blakely."

Miss Blakely says, "I'll be in touch about your case against the gang."

I nod. I'm not in the mood to think about it right now. I turn to Cleary. "Okay, I'm ready to go."

When we arrive back at the safe house, I say, "I'll fix lunch for us."

Hald smiles and responds, "Sounds good to me. Cleary, let's do our rounds."

When the officers leave to do their guarding routines, I fix a simple lunch of grilled cheese sandwiches, apple slices, and chocolate pudding. They return to the kitchen, and we eat.

Later in the afternoon, both officers' phones ring. They read the message and jump up. Officer Hald motions for me to get down on the floor, and to be quiet. I see Cleary do a fast run around the house checking doors and windows. I look at Hald with a question in my eyes. He whispers the safe house has been compromised.

I wonder what that means. Hald and Cleary are acting like it's an emergency. I can feel my anxiety rising as I sense their tension.

We wait in silence. We hear something at the back door. I watch Cleary move to the door and stand to the side with his gun raised. Hald is beside me with one hand on my shoulder and the other holding his gun.

The door opens slowly. We can hear Cleary demanding whoever it is to drop their gun. Then he yells out, "What the--"

***

"Don't shoot me, you idiot." I recognize Jones's voice.

"Detective Jones, why are you here? Are you alone? You're breaking protocol. Lower your weapon." Cleary sounds disgusted.

183

We hear the back door close. Jones, followed closely by Cleary, comes into the living room.

"Hi, Hald. Hi, Suzanne."

Hald says, "What're you doing here? We didn't call for backup. Put your gun away now."

"I know you guys are angry. I came to help. I was afraid I might be too late, so I didn't take the steps I should've taken." Jones replaces his gun in his holster.

Neither Cleary nor Hald has holstered his gun.

"Even if you mean to help, you know the drill. Sit down here, Jones."

Detective Jones sits in the easy chair Cleary indicates. Meanwhile Hald allows me to stand and move back to the couch. I'm very curious about this turn of events. Neither Cleary nor Hald has relaxed.

Jones slowly moves both his hands up and down in a calming motion. "Easy, guys, I didn't mean to startle you."

Cleary responds, "Then explain yourself."

"I saw the warning as did Forester. We split up and came to the safe houses to be certain everything is okay."

"What a load of crap. Watch him, Hald, I'll make the call."

"That's not necessary."

"You broke the rules."

Cleary comes back to the room a few minutes later. The three of us have been sitting in silence.

Cleary says, "No one seems to know you're whereabouts. You weren't sent here, and Forester did not show up at the other house."

Jones half rises from his seat. "What? I know we weren't sent here. But, where's Forester?" Either Jones is a good actor or he's genuinely surprised by this bit of news.

Cleary asks, "I repeat, why are you here?"

"We know there's a mole, and I want to find the traitor."

Hald jumps up. "You think it's Cleary or me?"

"We don't know who it is. We're trying to keep our witnesses safe."

"What do you think Cleary and I are doing?"

"I'm here to help."

"How do we know it's not you or Forester?"

Jones shrugs. "You don't, and I don't like this any better than you. It's the best plan I could come up with. Someone is dead serious, and it has to stop. If it's one of you guys or your replacements, it will be two against one with me here."

Hald says, "I don't like the way you're doing this."

Jones shrugs again. We resume sitting in silence. Everyone keeps eyeballing each other suspiciously. I can't take the tension.

I ask, "Can I say something?"

Cleary snaps, "What?"

"I'm going to my room. I need to scream or throw something. This tension is too much for me. And one more thing. Isn't it likely the mole is in the forensics department?"

Hald says, "Who knows? Please keep your door open so we can see you. We're still on alert."

"Will do."

I go to my room and plop down on the bed. *Why did Detective Jones break protocol? It's frightening to think someone I've come to trust might be trying to get rid of Gus and me. I wonder what's going on in the other safe house.* I return to the living room.

"Have any of you heard how Gus is?"

Cleary answers me without taking his eyes off Jones. "We can't communicate directly, but as far as we know, things are safe at the other house."

"Does anyone know if a date has been set for Gus's trial?"

Jones says, "No date, but his attorney is working to get the charges thrown out after your pretrial."

"Good, because he's innocent."

Jones makes a sound between a cough and a snort. "Obviously, as the fingerprints were the only evidence for him also."

"And for him, it's not even possible."

With eyebrows raised, Jones says, "What do you mean?"

Now all three men are looking at me. "I heard they're prints from both hands."

"Yeah."

"Gus is a left hander, and he severely burned his right hand. He slipped in the kitchen and grabbed a hot burner. On his right hand only the thumb has any print left."

Jones says, "I'll be damned. I wonder why this never came up before? He had to be fingerprinted when he was arrested."

"Maybe someone lied? Gus has full use of the hand. It's only the tips of his fingers which are scarred. I'd only started there when the accident happened. I learned how to cook to help him while he recovered."

Hald says, "What an interesting development."

"Like I said before, the evidence is pointing to the forensics department." No one responds, so I return to my room. Hopefully Gus will be able to get on with his dream. The day has taken its toll. I fall asleep and dream of being chased by a shadowy figure.

I awaken with a start. There's someone coming into my room, and I start to scream.

Cleary says, "It's okay, Suzanne. I'm checking to see if you're hungry. Supper is ready."

"Sorry, you fit right into my nightmare."

I look up to see Officer Hald and Detective Jones in the hall with their guns out. Feeling foolish, I follow the three men out to the kitchen. I see a plate of hot sandwiches and fruit.

We eat in silence. It appears none of the three trust the others. They keep their guns on the table, and there's no camaraderie like before. It's going to be a long evening. I wash the few dishes and tidy up the kitchen while the guys do their rounds. I feel like I'm walking on eggshells. I guess we're all paranoid.

I settle in the living room on a recliner and absent-mindedly page through a magazine I find on the coffee table. Hald is at the front window. Jones is in the dark kitchen staring out at the back yard. Cleary moves from one bedroom to another looking out the windows. Their vigilance lets me know they don't think the threat is gone.

Suddenly the lights go out, and Detective Jones yells, "Incoming. Cover your eyes."

Chapter 23

Hald leaps over the coffee table and pulls me out of the chair to the floor. Cleary runs out to the kitchen with Jones. There is a crash through the kitchen window, a bright light, and then a lot of smoke. It's like a thick fog. I hear gun shots.

Between the smoke and Hald on top of me, I can't see a thing. I hear the front door crash open and decide to be quiet in hopes whoever it is won't know where I am. Something warm is running down the side of my face.

There are several more shots. People are shouting, and I hear running. Then I hear something heavy fall close by. *What's happening?* Even if I wanted to move, I'm trapped.

I hear someone calling my name, but it's too muffled to tell who it is. I decide to remain silent until I'm sure I know who's speaking.

Whoever it is, they're getting closer. "What the hell are you doing here?" I think Jones is speaking, but I can't be sure.

"Where's Suzanne?" *Rob?*

"Answer my question first."

"I came to help. Where's Suzanne?"

Then I hear the detective say, "Oh hell, both Cleary and Hald have been injured. Suzanne must be under Hald. Help me move these guys."

My two guards have been shot, but Jones wasn't? Why is Rob here? How did he find the safe house? Something is terribly wrong.

"Suzanne, are you okay?" Rob asks as they lift Officer Hald off me. I slowly sit up. I look at both Jones and Rob. I look at their guns. When they see my gaze, both men holster their weapons.

As Jones bends down to take a closer look at Hald's injuries, he says, "I got the one shooter as he tried to go back outside. Thank God he couldn't find you."

Rob helps me get to my feet. I jerk away from him as I ask, "Who was it?"

"Satchi."

"Is he dead?"

"Yes."

"Good riddance." I close my eyes as a feeling of relief washes over me. I reopen them to see the nightmarish scene in front of me. I go over to see if I can be of help to Cleary and Hald. Both men appear to be unconscious. Cleary has a bullet wound in his chest. Hald wasn't shot, but he was hit on the back of his head.

Jones asks, "Are you okay? Are you hurt? You're covered in blood. You look like you might be in shock."

"I'm fine. We need to help these guys." I'm fighting with myself not to throw up at the sight of all the blood. I start to tremble.

Rob says, "Sit down, Suzanne. I'll get some towels, and I'll get you something to drink."

I nod. "Look around. You'll find towels in the bathroom."

I watch as Jones calls for an ambulance and back up. He puts his phone away. "You look worried."

Rob drops off a pile of towels, and I ask him to get ice for Hald's head injury. Rob nods and heads for the kitchen. I place towels on the officers's wounds and grab an extra towel to try to wipe the blood off my face. "To your question, Jones, sure I'm worried."

"About what? We got Satchi."

I say, "Yeah, and that's good. It's everything else starting with your arrival, Detective."

"You don't know who to trust?"

"Bingo."

"I spotted the guy in the backyard as he threw something toward the house. I called out so everyone would know. Cleary went back to the living room when we heard the front door open."

I remain silent. My mind is racing. *What am I supposed to do? I'm alone with the two men who aren't supposed to be here. And, if I understand the detective, there might be one more gunman out there somewhere, or, even worse, he's one or both of these guys.*

"Say something."

"Like what, Detective? The two officers, who didn't trust you, are now unconscious. A man, who's unconnected to your team, somehow found this 'safe house.' I may be with the very people who want to silence me."

"You've got it wrong."

"It's how I'm seeing it."

"Okay. I get it."

I sigh. "What happens now?"

"Help is on the way."

Rob comes in and hands me a glass of orange juice. "We need to talk."

"Okay. Explain why you're here at the same time as Satchi. Did you come together? Are you the second gunman? How did you find this place?"

Jones says, "Good questions, King. Answer her."

Rob presses a clean towel on Cleary's wound. "I didn't come with Satchi, and I'm not the other gunman. I didn't even see him."

"Don't bother going further. I won't believe anything you say."

Rob pauses. Then says, "Okay, maybe later."

Maybe never, I think. I get another towel for Hald's wound, hoping to stop his blood loss. Neither officer has regained consciousness. We wait in silence for the ambulance to get here. Jones keeps roaming the house looking out the windows. Finally we hear sirens. Once the paramedics and the police arrive, the detective makes his report. I listen but learn nothing. Afterwards he joins Rob and me. We are sitting quietly in the kitchen.

Jones gets a glass of water and sits down. "We can't stay here. We know there was one other intruder. We need to go now. And, King, you're coming too."

I shrug. "I'll get my stuff. I should just leave it packed."

After repacking I join the two men, and we go out to a van parked down the side street.

Rob asks, "Where're we going?"

"I have a place off everyone's radar. No one in the police department knows about it, not even my partner."

"Hard to do things secretly when you have a mole," I mutter.

Jones grunts. "Yes it is."

This is the sum total of our conversation. I know I'm not in the mood for small talk. All I can think about is how many people have died or been hurt trying to help me. My guilt is overwhelming. Eventually, Jones pulls up to a house. I know we're close to Shipley, but I've no idea of the exact location.

"You two stay here while I check the place out."

Rob turns in his seat and says, "I'm sorry I scared you by coming today."

"Okay." I know my tone is flat.

"You don't trust me now, do you?"

I shrug. "Everything keeps changing."

Jones comes back to the van, starts it up, and pulls into the garage. We dash out, per his instructions, and dart into the house. Once inside, the detective turns on the lights.

I ask, "Where are we?"

"We're in a rural area outside of town. This house belongs to an old friend of mine. He lets me use it when I need a place away. It's built like a fortress, including light-blocking shades and an alarm. I know it's drab and dark, but it should be safe. Also, no one leaves until we figure out what is going on."

I can't kick my diner routines. I ask, "What are we doing for meals?"

"I keep the place well stocked."

"Fresh food?"

"No, it's all frozen except for some snack stuff."

"That'll work. Where do I put my things?"

"All three bedrooms and the one bathroom are upstairs. Linens and towels are in the hall closet up there. Come on, I'll show you your rooms." The detective turns to Rob. "And I'm dead serious, you're not to leave."

"Don't worry. I've no intention of leaving Suzanne."

Chapter 24

We follow the detective upstairs. Jones assigns our bedroom. After unpacking, I plop down on the bed. The room is ugly with a faded flower wallpaper on all four walls, but at least the place is clean. I can put up with drab and ugly for safety's sake. I hope there are no mice. You never know in these old homes. There is a chest of drawers to the right of the door. The head of the bed is against the outside wall in the middle of the room. In the farthest right corner there is a lounge chair with a small bookcase next to it.

I hear Jones calling me. "Hey, Suzanne, feel like getting us something for supper?"

"Sure, Detective." I go downstairs and examine the large, eat-in kitchen. It reminds me of an old farm house. If we could raise the shades, it might even look homey. There's a large freezer in the pantry between the kitchen and the mud room. I find some meat and vegetables. I work on thawing it all out so I can cook. Dinner is ready about an hour and half after the request. I call the guys.

"This is great," says Rob.

Never looking up, I say, "I'm glad you like it." My tone is flat and uninviting.

No one says anything for the rest of the meal. When we finish eating, I begin to clear the table.

Rob says, "Let me help you with the clean-up."

"I prefer to do this alone. In fact, if you guys don't mind, I'll take care of the kitchen and all meal preps. I'll keep my room clean, and you two can keep the rest of the house tidy. Okay?"

The detective responds, "Works for me if it's what you want."

"It is." I turn to Rob. "Okay?"

He pauses, then he says, "Yeah, fine." His tone lets me know he's not pleased.

The two men move into the living room. I wash and dry the dishes, and then I look for any task to help me avoid joining the men in the other room. If I don't keep busy, I fear I'll start screaming. I finish the last of my chores. On the way out, I grab a bottle of wine, a corkscrew, and one glass.

Walking through the living room, I say good night without looking at either man. In my room there's a small bookcase. Luckily I find an interesting mystery. With the wine and a good book, my evening passes pleasantly.

***

At six the next morning, I go downstairs to fix breakfast. I've barely started when Rob joins me.

"I can't stand being shut out like this."

I shrug. "I can't stop you from talking."

"I wanted to be sure you were safe. I don't know who I can trust."

"I'm having the same problem."

"I started working for the Hoskins months ago. The case was cold, and the police were out of leads. Their son had mentioned to his parents he was hanging out with a guy he had met in Columbus. He also mentioned the man has a nasty facial scar. Turns out the two of them were planning a robbery. They had a falling out, and the other guy killed their son and got away.

"I thought I was on the right track when I found Satchi with his prominent facial scar. He had a long record of violence and robberies. I started tailing him. There was nothing out of the ordinary until shortly before he came here. It appeared he was recruiting guys for something. I made it a point for him to notice me. It worked. There were four of us all together. He said our job was to scare a few shop owners so they would sell their properties. He refused to tell us who we were working for except to say it was a guy with a lot of dough.

"He devised the extortion scheme shortly after we arrived and cased out the shops. I knew where you worked, but I didn't know how to stop Satchi without blowing my cover. The guy was bad news and had a ferocious temper. When the first shop owner refused to pay, he roughed him up pretty bad. But, I thought Satchi was going to kill the second guy. After they left him to die in the fire, I doubled back and pulled him out. Satchi found out and the three beat me up. Remember the night I came to your place?"

"I remember. Didn't you also tell me you trained those two new guys?" I'm still suspicious of how and why he came to the safe house. I'm thinking it may work to my advantage to keep him talking.

"Yeah, I did. But, I made sure Satchi selected guys who had outstanding warrants. I knew I'd turn them into the local law when the time was right."

"Clever. How did you find the safe house? And, Jones told me the second gunman went out the back. Satchi came in the front door and was shot by Cleary, but Cleary was shot in the back. And, Hald was hit on the back of his head."

"Yeah, I saw Jones come out. I'm not the second shooter."

197

"First Jones shows up unexpectedly, and both Cleary and Hald were upset with the way he came. Then you show up as all hell is breaking loose. Is it any wonder I don't trust either one of you?"

"After your trial, I knew something is rotten in the police department. I have a police radio and heard the warning. I spotted Jones and followed him. I don't know anything about why he came. I chose to stay outside to guard the house. I knew I wouldn't be welcome inside."

"Did you see two attackers?"

"No, I only saw the one. I started to go out back when I saw Jones run out. When I returned to the front of the house, I found Satchi dead."

"So, you don't know what happened in the house?"

"No."

"You know it almost sounds like you're trying to convince me the detective is the bad guy."

"I think so too, King." Detective Jones sits down at the table.

"I want Suzanne to know she isn't the only one with trust issues."

Now the detective is glaring at Rob. "What are you saying? Give it to me straight."

"Jones, you broke protocol, and anyone could have followed you like I did. And, both officers were attacked."

Jones jumps up. "I didn't shoot my fellow officers. I'm thinking you had a clean shot at Cleary when he turned back to check on me. I'm still not convinced you aren't the second shooter."

I decide to intervene before they come to blows. "I guess it's clear none of us trust the others. How long do we have to stay here?"

Jones takes a sip of coffee. "We're staying here until I know the coast is clear."

I ask, "Have you heard anything about Gus?"

"I'm assuming he's okay. No news is generally good news in these situations."

I finish eating and tidy up the kitchen. Once again I don't want to hang out with the gruesome twosome, so I go back to my room. I feel like I'm in jail. I pick up the book I'm reading and settle in for a long day. Around noon I set out a simple lunch and repeat my routine with supper. Conversation is limited at these meals, but there's no more arguing. After the final cleanup, which I drag out as long as possible, I grab a clean glass. There is still wine in the bottle I left in my room. If this keeps up much longer, I'll have to get treatment for alcoholism.

Back in my room, I begin to read. An hour later the lights go out. I sit absolutely still. *Oh no, now what? What am I supposed to do? Should I try to find one of the guys? Or is one of them making his move?* Heart-pounding fear keeps me frozen in my seat. I hear my door opening slowly.

"Suzanne?" Rob whispers into my dark room.

I'm too scared to answer. I hear him enter and softly close the door. Then he turns on a flashlight. So much for remaining hidden.

"There you are." In an instant he's kneeling by my chair.

"What's going on?" I ask stiffly.

"I don't know, but I'm expecting the worst. Jones is checking it out. I told him I was coming up here with you."

"I thought no one knew about this place."

Rob nods and says, "Me, too. Did you use your phone?"

"No. It's a burner phone, and I haven't turned it on. Did you contact anyone?"

"No, and Jones says he hasn't either. What are you doing up here?"

I gesture towards my book and glass. "I'm reading and drinking wine, or was until the lights went out."

"Do you have an extra glass?"

"No, but feel free to drink from the bottle."

He takes the bottle, and has several gulps. We sit in silence listening for any clues as to what might be happening. Then the lights flash on.

A minute or so later, Detective Jones comes to the door. He knocks and then enters. "We appear to have blown a fuse. Luckily I found an extra one on top of the box. I see no signs of unwanted visitors."

I guess it's my nerves or maybe the wine, but I start to laugh and can't stop. Pretty soon Rob and the detective join in.

When we start to settle down, the detective says, "Is this a private party, or can I join you?

"You're welcome, but we have no glasses and Rob is drinking straight out of the bottle, which is getting low."

"I'll be right back."

After Jones leaves, I say, "We could move downstairs, Rob."

"Nah, I like it here." As if to prove his point, he settles back using the bed as a back rest.

"Okay, guys, I come bearing gifts." The detective returns with one glass, another bottle of wine, and a bag of pretzels. He brought a soft drink for himself. Without hesitation, we jump right in. We're enjoying a strained congeniality when we hear the back door alarm. Detective Jones jumps up.

"Stay here, King, I'm going down. Keep alert."

I say, "Will this nightmare ever end?"

"Shh..."

Chapter 25

We wait and listen for several agonizing minutes. At last we hear footsteps, but then we hear multiple footsteps coming up the stairs. I see Rob go to the side of the door where he is out of sight of anyone coming in. He reaches over and turns out the light. I slide out of the chair to the floor. Now kneeling by the bed, I decide to send up a prayer.

Detective Jones walks in, flips on the light, and is followed by Officers Bates and Miles. All three turn when Rob moves into sight.

"Who're your friends, Jones?" Rob has not holstered his gun but is pointing it down.

"Rob King, meet Officers Karen Bates and Chuck Miles."

Rob responds, "I thought no one else knew about this place."

I'm thinking the same thing, and I notice Rob is staying out of their striking range. I get up and sit on the bed. Here we go with yet another explanation differing from the original plan.

Jones says, "Put your gun down. These are the good guys. I called for their help. I need to have people I trust beside me. King, we both need to sleep. They're our night shift."

Bates smiles and says, "Hi, Suzanne."

I nod to the two officers."Hi. I wish I could say I'm glad to see you, but I'm having trouble understanding all the rule changes."

"We understand, as we feel the same way," responds Miles.

"Yet, here you are as a result of a phone call no one was supposed to make. I guess the rules are only for me."

"I see where you're coming from, if Jones didn't tell you we were coming. I'm here because I trust my partner, Bates, and Jones. We've been through a lot together these past six years, and..." Miles appears uncomfortable with whatever he was going to say.

"And?" I prompt.

"We like you, Suzanne. You've been through a lot, yet you haven't given up. Also, you've remained loyal to your friend, Gus. We want to help you guys."

Apparently Rob is not satisfied with Miles's answer. "Jones, you said no calls. How can you be sure your whereabouts haven't been given away?"

"Fair enough. First, I made the call before we left the other safe house. I used special codes, and these two officers have been here before. I know I told you no one else was aware of the existence of this place. I should have told you the truth. I disposed of my burner phone at the other place. And second, these officers know how to lose any tails."

I ask, "How can we trust you, if you keep changing your story?" I shift in my seat, feeling frustrated. "Have you guys uncovered the identity of the mole?"

Bates answers as she sits on the opposite side of the bed. "Not yet."

"Funny how all your safe houses are known. Why have them?" I ask.

Jones frowns and shakes his head. "It's not funny to us."

"Any word about Gus?"

Miles answers, "The other safe house wasn't attacked. Gus is fine."

"I'm glad, but it makes no sense."

Jones asks, "Why?"

"Why do they keep coming after me? I know nothing, and I've nothing to sell. Gus has already agreed to sell the diner. What else is left?"

There is silence for a few seconds, and then Jones says, "Maybe they think you do know something or have found whatever it is they want."

"Well, they're wrong. I wish I knew what the paperwork from the bag concerned. There's a piece missing, and it's driving me crazy. Did you ever find the contents?"

Jones shakes his head. "Nope, still missing."

"You told us a member of the forensics team told you about the contents. And then, another guy in the department reported no contents but did find our fingerprints. Are you investigating your forensics department?"

Rob says, "She's right. Everything keeps going back to them. Jones, are you even considering your mole is there?"

"Of course we are. But, there're three people in the department. Which one is the culprit, or is it the whole team? Suspecting and proving it are two different things. And what's the motive?"

No one has an answer. Bates and Miles leave to begin their shifts. Once it's just the three of us, I resume the conversation. "What are we going to do, Jones?"

"What do you mean?"

"I want to get on with my life, and I'm sure Gus feels the same way. How do we end this standoff?"

"I'm out of ideas," Jones says yawning and stretching. "I need sleep. Let's talk about it tomorrow." He nods and leaves the room.

Rob and I say goodnight. I'm hoping one of us will come up with a plan during the night.

***

I get up early to begin breakfast. Bates and Miles drift in and out on their rounds. After a while, Jones and Rob join me at the table. We focus on eating. Then, I break the silence to share an idea.

"Someone seems to want to silence me. What if we make it easy for them to get to me? What if we set a trap?"

Rob shakes his head. "No, Suzanne, you aren't trained for what you're suggesting."

"Something has to give. What we're doing now is running from place to place. It's crazy. Rob, you've your work to do, the police have their duties, and I don't want to spend my days hiding. I need to make a living."

Rob puts his hand over mine. "But, offering yourself as bait might get you killed."

"If I don't, how long will this go on? How many other people will be hurt?" I slip my hand out of his grasp. "Do you have another idea?"

Jones finally weighs in. "Let me think this over."

Rob looks at Jones as if he's seeing something horrifying. "You can't be considering this lunacy, Jones. You're going to get her killed. Or is that what you really want?"

I won't be stopped. "Go cool off, Rob. Detective, I appreciate your willingness to consider my idea. Let me know when you're ready to talk."

After Jones and Rob leave, I work at cleaning up the kitchen and preparing the menus for the day. When I finish with the work, I settle down in the living room to wait.

I begin to think about offering myself as bait. I have to admit, it scares me. But, I really want to find out who is behind all this and why. Bottom line, I refuse to live my life feeling helpless any longer. I'm ready whenever they are.

About an hour later Detective Jones and Officers Bates and Miles join me.

Bates says, "I'd say you're feeling better, Suzanne."

I smile. "I am. Detective, have you thought about what I proposed?"

The two officers turn towards the detective. Curiosity is evident in their expressions.

Jones says, "Suzanne has suggested setting a trap using her as bait, and I think she might be on to something. We're running out of leads."

"Well that's true enough." Miles says. "So far neither Todd, Luke, or John Doe have talked. It's like they're confident we can't touch them."

Jones pauses then nods. "The way I'm seeing it, we need leverage. And this may be the way to get it."

I nod along with him. "Let's start planning before I lose my nerve."

Rob joins our group. For the next hour we brainstorm how we'll set our trap. Rob doesn't speak. He sits silently looking down at his hands. Once we all, except Rob, agree on a plan, Bates and Miles go upstairs to sleep. They go back on shift at ten tonight.

I go out to the kitchen to get lunch. Rob and Jones remain in the living room, but I can hear their conversation.

"King, this plan is good."

"But it's not foolproof. She could get hurt or worse."

"I can't argue, but we're running out of choices. We could use your help with this as we're short-handed. But, even if you won't join us, we're going forward."

"I won't support what could turn out to be her death sentence."

I hear someone stomp upstairs, and then a door slams. The detective comes out to the kitchen. We eat, and he leaves to continue his rounds. About twenty minutes later, Rob comes in.

"Suzanne, we need to talk."

"Let me guess. This means you want me to see something from your point of view and not mine."

"You bet I do. This whole trap scheme stinks. So many things can go wrong."

"I realize it's not perfect. But so far the bad guys have been winning. Maybe by doing something unexpected, we can cause them to make a mistake. I'm tired of feeling like a victim."

"I've participated in undercover work. It's impossible to anticipate every possibility."

"Okay, I get it, but I still believe it's worth a try."

"I don't think you realize the risk you would be taking. But why am I surprised? You're a two-bit waitress in a podunk town. You live in a fairy tale."

"Why don't you tell me how you really feel? Oh wait, you just did. Get out of my sight."

"Suzanne, I'm sorry. I just wanted.--"

"Pulverize me with words, and then you think a little apology will make it better? GET OUT." I realize I'm shouting. I'm so angry, I want to throw something. I begin to look around.

Jones comes in. "What's going on?"

I stop the search, and spit out, "Rob thinks I'm stupid, cheap, and helpless. I was asking him to go away."

"That's not what I said."

"Maybe not the exact words, but it's the drift. GET OUT."

"King, we're moving forward with this plan. You can join us or get out of our way. It's your choice."

"I refuse to be a part of this lunacy. I'm out of here."

"You're not leaving this house. In fact, give me your phone. I won't let you sabotage our plans."

Rob tosses his phone to Jones. We hear him stomp upstairs.

"Are you okay, Suzanne?"

"Peachy. I'm going to my room. I'll come back down later to make supper." Then it's my turn to stomp out.

The rest of the day passes quietly. A little after nine, the two officers join us. We work on finessing our plan. I find forcing myself to focus on every single detail is helping to keep my mind off the earlier scene. We decide we'll begin tomorrow.

I go up to bed feeling exhausted. Rob's words are still ringing in my ears. *Why was he so mean? Is this the real Rob? I hope I'm finally trusting the right people. My life depends on it.*

Chapter 26

The next morning I wake up at 6:15. After showering, dressing, and packing, I go down to fix breakfast. The plan is for me to return home after we eat. I'm ready, I hope.

Before leaving, I say good-bye to the detective and Officer Miles. When Bates drops me off at my house, she opens her door, stands, and half pleads, "Suzanne, we want to keep you safe. This is a huge mistake moving back home. Please call if you need us."

"It's my life, and I'll live it like I want. I can take care of myself," I yell while entering the house. From the front window, I watch as the officer gets back in her car and shakes her head like I'm the biggest fool she has ever met. Then she backs out of the driveway and is gone. Hopefully someone saw our little scene.

As soon as I'm inside, I thoroughly check the entire house. Now my job is to wait. Nothing makes more noise than an empty house. I try to stay busy so as not to have a nervous breakdown.

It's not too bad during the day, but, as it gets dark, I can't stop myself from worrying. I close the curtains and blinds and check all the locks. After dinner, I pour myself a glass of wine and settle on the couch. Chances are good no one will come tonight. They might not even know I'm back yet, or they might be doing their own reconnaissance.

I wake up the next morning still on the couch and realize: I'm alive and I'm alone. Those facts aren't bad considering the alternatives. I fix myself some cereal and lots of coffee.

Later in the morning, I walk to the grocery store to restock my shelves. I may be a two-bit waitress, but I do know how to cook. As I walk home with my purchases, I try to keep my focus on planning menus rather than thinking about who might be watching me. I breathe a sigh of relief when I'm back home.

I keep busy cleaning and cooking. My job is to be inside this house. I'm the bait. I can only trust everyone else is doing their part.

Three days go by. There have been no unwanted visitors. Was our plan discovered? I promised there would be no contact unless I'm attacked. I must continue my routine until I hear differently. Well, one good thing is my house hasn't been this clean in years. And, I've prepared enough frozen meals to last me weeks. If I stay here, maybe I should get a dog.

On the fifth day in the early morning, all hell breaks loose. I've become braver and am sleeping upstairs in my new bedroom. Around 2:30 a.m. the clatter of cans getting kicked wakes me up. Those empty cans are my burglar alarm. I placed them at both doors and on the windowsills downstairs. Someone has stumbled on them. I get up and grab a wooden baseball bat I found when cleaning out one of the closets. I'm now regretting not accepting the gun Jones offered.

Positioning myself at the side of the door like Rob did, I raise the bat over my head and tell myself to swing down hard and fast, as I'll be up against a gun. I pray I won't drop it due to my nervousness. I hear one set of footsteps coming up the stairs. He sounds like he's trying to be as quiet as possible. Earlier I closed all the doors up here. Now I hear him opening each one. There will be three before this room. My doorknob starts to slowly turn. I ready myself. The door quietly pushes open. A gun appears. I smack the wrist with every ounce of strength I have. The gun goes off and slightly dips down. I take one step forward and quickly draw the bat back and swing straight at the intruder as he comes in. I hear a crack, a yelp of pain, and a muffled curse. Whoever it is has fallen back into the hall. I bolt out the door dragging the bat with me, and give the shooter a final slug with the bat to get him out of my way. I run downstairs and dash out the front door. Officer Bates grabs me and points out the car I'm to get into. Then she enters the house. Miles is close behind her. I run to the car, jump in, and lock the doors. I begin to pray for the officers now trying to capture the gunman alive.

It seems like forever before I see Bates and Miles half carry, half drag someone out. Now I'm to leave the car so they can get him down to the station for questioning.

I return to the house, collapse on the couch, tremble and start to cry. Bates comes back in and goes upstairs. When she returns, she asks me the whereabouts of the bat. I tell her I left it in the front seat of the car as directed. She comes over and sits next to me. She shows me the gun in the bag. Then she puts her arm around my shoulder.

"You did well, Suzanne. You have a powerful swing."

"I played softball all through high school. I've never hit anyone before, but I wanted to stop him."

"And, you did. I think his arm is broken, and he might have some fractured facial bones. I can tell you he's not feeling too good."

"At least we got him alive. Do you recognize him?"

"No, but we'll run his fingerprints. Thanks for your willingness to catch him in the act. I need to get this gun to Miles to take down to the station. Then I'll resume my post outside."

"Surely there aren't any more gunmen out there tonight?"

"Probably not, but Miles and I will finish our shift. We're not going to take any chances. Lock up when I leave."

"I will, and thanks for all your help."

I carefully relock both doors and reset my can alarms. I know I can't sleep yet, so I make some hot chocolate, turn out the lights, and sit in the dark. On the surface it looks like our plan has worked. Now, will Jones be able to get one of these guys to talk?

***

Later in the day Detective Jones drops by the house. He looks tired. "You did well, slugger."

I smile and say, "Who was the guy? Any luck getting the name of the kingpin?"

"Not yet, but we haven't given up. This latest guy is Jake Pearson. We now have four guys in custody. We'll keep working on them. A connection is bound to surface. Have you heard from Rob?"

"No, and I don't want to hear from him. He let me know what he thinks about me, and I now know his act with me was all part of his cover."

"I'm not his fan, either. But, back to the other problem. We can't guarantee there won't be another attempt on your life. Someone appears desperate, and they apparently have deep pockets. Are you sure you won't take a gun?"

I chuckle and say, "Right before I used the bat, I thought a gun might be better. With my luck though, I'd probably shoot myself. Thanks anyway."

"Well then here's one of the bats we use in our softball games. We have to keep your bat as evidence. Please don't take any chances."

"I'll be careful. Have you heard anything about Gus?"

213

"His pretrial is next week. Should go quickly and in his favor, as yours did."

After the detective leaves, I begin job hunting on the internet. The search is frustrating, as there's nothing appealing to me. I feel emotionally drained. I reset my burglar alarms and go to bed early. I know part of my exhaustion is from my deep sadness over losing Rob. I was hoping we could make things work. But, it was a fantasy. Now, it's no Gus, no Rob, and an uncertain future.

Chapter 27

I startle awake to the clanging of cans. I'm instantly alert. It sounds like the front door. I grab the bat and get ready for another fight. Unlike last night, this person ignores the other doors and comes straight to my room. As it opens, I swing hard. I hear a crack and a piercing cry of pain.

"What the hell? You broke my arm. Turn on the light, Suzanne."

Flipping the switch, I demand, "Rob, what're you doing here?"

"I came to check on you. I thought you'd still be up. Are you okay?"

"Try again, Rob. I still have a bat."

"I want to apologize again. I'm sorry for what I said."

"I'm not buying it. Do you have a weapon?"

"Yes, but not to use against you. Did you just hear something?"

"That will be the police."

Miles runs in. "What are you doing here, King? You were told to stay at the house."

"I came to help. I made a terrible mistake not joining you guys from the beginning. Jones stopped by this afternoon. He said the plan worked and Suzanne handled herself well."

Miles frowns. "I can't imagine Jones said it was okay for you to come here. I'm calling him." Miles takes a step out in the hallway to make the call.

"I think you broke my arm."

"I'm sorry I hurt you, but you shouldn't walk into my house like you own it. Your actions are suspicious as well as annoying as hell."

Miles rejoins us. "Jones didn't give you permission to come here. He wants to talk to you." He hands Rob the phone.

Rob says, "Hello." He's unable to say anything else as we hear yelling on the other end. Then he says, "Yes, I know I disobeyed your orders, but I meant no harm. I wanted to help. Yes, I understand. I can't talk more, I need to get some medical care." Rob hangs up rapidly. "Suzanne, will you take me to the E.R.?"

Miles says, "I'll drop you off."

"I prefer Suzanne. She broke it."

"It's okay, Miles, I'll take him. Rob, meet me downstairs." I quickly dress and take him to the hospital.

Two hours later we exit. Rob has a cast and a sling on his right arm. He smiles and asks, "Are you hungry?"

"You just left the E.R., and you want to eat?"

"Yes."

I sigh. "How about Hamburger Haven?"

"Perfect."

I drive to the restaurant where we use the drive-thru window. When we get back to my place, I carry the bags into the kitchen. After we eat, I consent to let him stay the night in the bedroom he used before.

"Rob, stay in your room and out of mine. I still have the bat."

"Okay. They gave me some pain pills which will knock me out anyway. You're safe."

I go to my room and firmly close the door.

After breakfast the next day I ask Rob to go back to Jones's safe house, to give me his key, and not to enter without my permission. He tries to apologize again for what he said.

"I'm sorry I broke your arm, but I can't forget what you said. We both need to move on. Go find the guy who murdered that poor family's son."

"It was Satchi. I got the evidence I needed against him and the other two guys."

"Well, good. But, whatever, you need to get on with your work. I've things to do, too."

"Like what?"

"Good-bye, Rob."

"We can still make this work."

I sigh, turn, and hold the door open for his exit. He stares at me, then finally starts to leave. As he passes me, he bends down and kisses my cheek. I firmly close the door. Then I let my tears flow.

Chapter 28

Later in the week I'm contacted by Gus's attorney. He wants me to testify at the pretrial. I eagerly agree to do so and remind him the fingerprints on record of Gus's right hand are bogus. He already knew, but he thanked me.

The bank calls and tells me I didn't qualify for the business loan. However, I won't give up. Doing an internet search, I learn of a grant for young women entrepreneurs. After reading for several hours about the grant and starting a business, I realize I'm hungry.

I decide to pack a lunch and eat in the park, as the day is sunny and bright with no wind. Picking out a bench where I can watch children playing on the swings and slides, I settle in.

A few minutes later Miss Blakely sits next to me. "I like to take a walk after lunch before returning to work. I saw you sitting here and wanted to say hello. How're your wounds healing?"

"Pretty good, thanks. I'm taking it a day at a time. How have you been?"

"I'm good. My business has picked up, thanks to your case. Detective Jones and others have been referring people to me."

"Great. At least I'm good for something."

"Whoa. You sound bitter."

"Well, you know Rob was using me as part of his undercover work. Since then he's let me know he has a poor opinion of me."

"He is a confusing guy."

I grimace. "It was all an act. He insulted me, and it hurt."

"I'm sorry. I hear you helped the police catch another gunman."

"Yeah, it was wild."

"Sounded terrifying. You were brave to stick your neck out."

"Now, if we can find out the name of the boss. We need answers."

"I know you do. I hear Detective Jones is relentless in getting information. If anyone can do it, he can."

"I hope so."

Miss Blakely nods and smiles. "So, what's next for you?"

"Well, there's a grant I'm researching. I might be able to go into business for myself if I qualify. I spent the morning working on it."

"Fantastic. Are you thinking of getting a diner?"

"I was, but now I'm leaning toward my own catering business. If I stay in Shipley, I could work out of my house. Gus doesn't want me to return to Indianapolis."

"Don't give up on Gus. Have you looked at other places?"

"Yeah, I've been doing my homework. It's a little overwhelming, but it's interesting."

"It sounds interesting and complex. I wish you the best, especially after everything you have been through. You're an awesome young woman."

"Thank you, Miss Blakely. You're making me feel better."

"Good, and please call me Marie. I have to get back to work. Good luck with your grant application."

She has put a long-lasting smile on my face. I finish lunch and return home to my computer. About mid afternoon, I get a call from Rob.

"What do you want?"

"Hi, Suzanne. I was thinking about you. If you aren't busy Saturday night, I'd like to take you to dinner."

"You mean like a date?"

"Exactly like a date."

"No, thank you."

"Let's start over."

"Not a good idea, Rob. Good-bye."

After I hang up, I argue with myself for a while and decide he's up to something. If I get involved with him again, it'll never work. I need a clean break. At least that's what my mind says, my heart is not so easy to convince.

*****

I continue working on the grant application the next morning. The process seems endless. I'll need to supply a complete business plan by the deadline in thirty days.

Taking a break, I walk over to the diner. It's so sad to see all the closed shops on this block. I want to see them open for business, especially Gus's Place. Something has to go right one of these days. Continuing on my walk, I end up in front of the newspaper office and go inside.

"May I help you?" A young woman about my age looks up from her terminal.

"Is John Burton in?"

She pauses and then says, "The photographer?"

"Yes."

"May I tell him who wants to see him?"

"Suzanne Moore."

She quickly gets up and goes into an office at the rear of this large room. She returns with an older man. This isn't John. My guess is he's a manager or something.

"Miss Moore, I'm Jim Lee. Why do you want to speak with John?"

"I want to ask him a couple questions about a story he was working on a while back."

"John isn't here today. If you leave your questions with me, I'll see to it he gets your message."

"Why didn't you say he's not here in the first place?"

"We're trying to be helpful."

I'm feeling impatient. "Tell him to call me. Here's my number." I grab a piece of paper and write out my contact information and hand it to Mr. Lee and leave. I find their behavior puzzling. Maybe John is still hiding because he knows something. The answers are always out of reach.

On the walk home, I try to figure out how to find the elusive photographer. And then it hits me--use a private investigator. Seems I have a one-track mind. I call Rob.

"Suzanne, is everything okay?"

"We need to talk."

"I'll be right over."

"Are you at home?"

"Yeah, do you want to come here?"

"No, meet me at Burger Haven in half an hour. This isn't a date."

"Okay, I'll be there."

At the restaurant, I explain wanting to hire him to find the photographer. While he eats, I explain my theory as to why John is still hiding. Rob listens without interrupting.

When I'm finally done talking, he takes a long drink of his iced tea. "Let me get this straight. You don't want anything to do with me, but you want to hire me to find this photographer."

"Correct. I'm trying to be efficient and not waste any more time."

He's quiet for a while. Then he says, "So, I'm not good enough to be your boyfriend, but I'm okay as a P.I.?"

"Correct. This is business not friendship. You're a private investigator familiar with the case, and you seem to know how to get what you want from people. If you don't want the job, I'll find someone else."

"You really know how to sweep a guy off his feet."

I frown. "I intend to get to the bottom of this mess. It isn't my idea of fun. My life has been turned upside down. Even if you won't help, I'll see this through somehow."

He moves his hands up and down in a calming motion. "Okay, okay. I'll help you. You're right, the cops don't seem to be making much headway. Trying to find the missing photographer makes sense. Do you have any ideas?"

"Well, I left a message at the newspaper for him to call me. But, I'll be shocked if he does. The people at his office didn't seem happy I was asking about him."

"Let's go back to your place and do some internet research on this guy."

"How about you go home and use your own computer?"

Rob sighs. "Strictly business, eh?"

"Yes."

"Then you owe me for this business lunch. Pay up. I get business expenses paid as part of my fee, which we haven't even discussed. As a matter of fact, I should have you sign a contract. You seem a little confused as to what you want from me."

I chuckle as I give him twenty dollars. "Keep the change."

"What change?"

***

Once I return home, I get back on the computer. First search is for Rob Clinger. He is from Kingston and has an address there. He has no history of problems noted. He sounds legitimate. I smile with relief, shake my head, and begin looking for info on the photographer. I do find some personal data on John Burton, but nothing to help me pinpoint his current location. Around mid-afternoon, I get a call from an unknown number.

"Hello."

"Suzanne?"

"Yes. Who is this?"

"You left a message to call."

Suddenly I recognize his voice. "John, why did you go into hiding?"

"After Jessica was killed, I was afraid I'd be next."

"Was Jessica having an affair with Reis?"

"Heavens no. But, she did know him. How did you find out?"

"Trying to put bits and pieces together. Reis is buying Gus's Place. Did she ever find out why Reis wanted the property?"

"Yeah, it has something to do with an inheritance. Reis seems to think a relative has cheated him. Amy Johnstone, who owned the gift shop, was involved somehow."

"Do you think Amy was related to Reis?"

"I don't know for sure. Jessica became convinced the family history should be our next step. We were going to try to put more of it together, but she was killed before we could."

"Do you have any idea as to who murdered her?"

"No. By the time I arrived at eight that morning, she was already dead and no one was there. I decided to run."

"Did you find out anything else?"

"Jessica had a hunch whatever Reis wanted was in the tunnels."

"How did she know about the tunnels?"

"Everyone from around here knows about the tunnels. Jessica was sharp, only she didn't have time to put it all together."

"Sounds like it was never the interstate access."

"No. Reis and maybe his family seems to be the story. I'm convinced Reis is behind all this."

I sigh and ask, "I agree, but how do we prove it?"

"I wish I knew. Listen, I hope my boss didn't scare you. He was trying to protect me and didn't realize we had met. He's the only one who knows how to reach me. I wish I knew more, so I could help you. Be careful."

"Thanks for calling. You've been a great help. You be safe, too."

After I hang up, I think over what we discussed. Could this be the missing piece? Obviously whoever is behind all this, believes he is going after something very valuable. But, what is *it?* Then I call Rob to let him know about this conversation.

"It definitely keeps pointing to Reis," Rob says when I finish.

"But, how do we prove it?"

"Not sure, but keep researching him. I want to do some checking on that forensics department. Then, let's compare notes. Be sure your doors and windows are locked."

After I hang up, I check all the locks and reset my burglar cans.

Chapter 28

Gus's pretrial is the following day. When I arrive at the courthouse, I discover his attorney has been successful in getting all charges dismissed. Getting ready to leave again, I see Detective Jones come out of the courtroom and ask about his progress finding the mole.

"So far, no luck."

"How frustrating."

"Yeah, sometimes it's harder to find someone when they're hiding in plain sight. It's even tougher since it's a member of our team. I've got to go. Be careful."

***

Later in the afternoon, I decide to call my former co-worker, Cheryl. She and Amy Johnstone had been close friends, and we haven't talked since the diner closed. Cheryl answers right away, and we make plans for tomorrow with lunch at her place. The rest of the day passes quietly.

***

Cheryl lives alone in a cute two-bedroom unit in an apartment house about a block from the town square. It's an easy three block walk from my house.

We talk casually and catch up with each other's activities. I totally downplay mine. Then I steer the conversation to the restaurant and the trouble of the closing of all the shops, which brings us to Amy.

I begin, "All those weeks we thought Amy was on vacation, and she was dead. Gives me the creeps."

Cheryl nods and wipes a tear away. "Me, too. She was so sweet. Who would do something so awful?"

"Do you know if she was seeing anyone?"

"She didn't date much, but a relative came into her life a little before she went missing."

"Did you meet this relative?"

Cheryl is quiet for a while. Then she says, "No, and she never told me his name. It was kind of confusing. She seemed happy, at first. I thought she didn't talk about him because she didn't want to jinx it. But then I knew something wasn't right."

"What do you mean?"

"It started innocent enough. Amy said he came into the store one day, and they hit it off. She said she never knew you could feel close to someone so quickly."

"But, it wasn't a love at first sight kind of thing?"

"No, this guy was some kind of relative. She talked about him like you would a long-lost brother. At least, she did at first. Then I noticed she seemed to be losing patience with him. She never said what turned her off, but she did mention he was on some kind of treasure hunt and wanted to dig up her basement."

"Treasure hunt? I wonder what that meant?"

"Don't know. Amy talked about how she was told her great grandfather had always been moaning about a lost treasure to anyone who would listen. She said she hated crybabies, and this guy was turning into one. I kept looking for him then."

"Did you ever see him?"

"I saw some distinguished-looking guy go into her shop several times. I assumed he was the one, but I don't know for sure."

"Did you ever see him again?"

"Yeah, I did. He met with Gus at the diner one day after hours."

I frown. "I don't remember that meeting."

"You had a hair appointment and had left early."

My mind is buzzing. *Could Amy be one of Reis's relatives? Wait a minute, am I now getting Cheryl into trouble? I need to keep Cheryl safe. Her life could be threatened if Reis finds out she recognizes him and can connect him to Amy.* Not wanting to alarm Cheryl, but desperate to keep her safe, I try to think of a subtle way to warn her. "This is off topic, but are you taking any vacations this year, Cheryl?"

Cheryl gives me a questioning look. "Where did that come from? But, yeah, I'm going away. This morning I made plans to go see my mom down in Orlando."

I smile. "Sounds like fun. When are you going?"

"I'm leaving the day after tomorrow. I'll be gone for about two weeks, although it might be longer. I'm thinking of looking for a job while I'm down there.

I feel relieved. "What a super idea. I hope you have a great time."

We spend the next couple hours giggling and talking about the people who used to come to Gus's Place. She's as sentimental about the restaurant as I am. I'm enjoying our time together. I leave around four and walk the three blocks to my house. I know it's not smart to be out alone, but I'm glad I talked with Cheryl. I keep wondering how this piece about Reis fits. I have a feeling it might be important. The part about Reis looking for a treasure is especially intriguing. I decide to call Rob.

"Hey, Rob."

"You sound funny. Are you outside?"

"Yeah, I had lunch with Cheryl."

"You shouldn't be out alone. You're going to get yourself killed."

"Calm down. I'm not arguing, but I hate being stuck at home all the time. I thought it'd be safer if I talk with you as I walk. I'm at my house now."

"Check it out thoroughly."

"Okay, give me five minutes."

"Don't hang up. Keep talking to me, so I know you're safe."

I hurriedly search the house. I recheck all the locks, look in closets, behind curtains, and under the beds. I reset my burglar cans. "All is well. I guess I'll say goodbye."

"Hold on. What were you doing out?"

"I told you. I had lunch with Cheryl."

"Who?"

"Cheryl, the other waitress at the diner. You know her. She has light brown hair and a bubbly personality."

"Oh, her. Why did you go over there?"

"She knew the shop owner who was murdered."

"Amy Johnstone?"

"Yeah. Cheryl told me Amy was friendly with Reis. But more than that, they were related somehow. They got together before he met Gus."

"Interesting. Did she say anything else?"

"Amy said Reis was looking for a treasure and thought it was somewhere in the tunnel."

"What kind of treasure?"

"She didn't know, and she didn't want him digging in her part of the tunnel."

"We're getting close. I can feel it. Good catch, Suzanne. But, please quit going out alone. Call me, I'll be happy to go with you."

"Goodbye, Rob." I hang up feeling irritated. *Who does he think he is asking so many questions and bossing me around? He works for me.*

***

231

The next morning I call Detective Jones to let him know about my conversation with Cheryl. He thanks me for keeping him informed. Then, I decide to call Rob again.

"Hi, Suzanne."

"I talked with Detective Jones. They still haven't identified the mole. And, I told him about my conversation with Cheryl."

"Good, I think. Are you positive you can trust Jones?"

"I'm growing more trusting of him. I'm not sure yet about you. We need help solving this mess, so I'm taking chances in the hope some answers will break loose."

"I understand. I'll let you know when I have something. Did you do any research on Reis's family?"

"Not yet, but I'll start now."

I return to my computer. The robbery took place in 1921. Reis wasn't born yet. I log on to an ancestry website and type in Reis's name. It takes awhile, but I find both sets of his grandparents. I then go to public records and research these grandparents. His paternal grandparents were divorced in 1920. They must have been wealthy, because they had many real estate holdings.

I later discover these same grandparents purchased the plot of land where the diner sits today. I'm feeling encouraged learning this information. The research takes all day with breaks for food. I finally call it quits.

***

Despite Rob's warning and my own misgivings, I decide I need to be brave, so the next morning I go back to the library to check the archives on the divorce of Reis's grandparents. I never dreamed I'd find so much. Article after article paints a picture of deceit and lots of rancor in this very public divorce. Carl Reis was the mayor of Shipley for eight years. So, when he divorced, it was big news. And, it sounds like Myrtle and Carl Reis were out for blood. They fought in court over everything, including their three children--one son and two daughters. Carl owned a jewelry store, and Myrtle was a nurse in the clinic. She never remarried and died in a car wreck about ten years after the divorce. Carl remarried and fathered another daughter. He died from a heart attack in 1940.

I'd heard there might have been a will in the bag found in the tunnel. I wonder whose it was and what properties it covered. Could the grandchildren be fighting over this one piece of land? Why would they? This block of land couldn't be the treasure someone is so desperate to get.

When I get back home from lunch, an idea blossoms. Even though I'm afraid it's hopeless, I call Gus. Maybe time has healed his anger with me.

"Hi, Gus. I have an idea I want to run by you. Please, hear me out and don't hang up."

"I'm listening, but I'm not promising anything."

"If it helps, I broke up with Rob. You were right, he was using me. But, he's a private investigator. He was working undercover, and I was never a part of it. I'd never betray you."

"I'm sorry you got used. But, for all you knew at first, Rob was a member of the gang."

"No argument there. By the way, is Reis still going to buy your diner?"

"Yes. I'm going to the diner tomorrow to box up the rest of my things. I'll be selling all the miscellaneous kitchenware I no longer want to a guy in Piqua."

"Okay, there's something else. I may be mistaken, but I think there's more to your picture of the Reds. "

"That's not new. You said the same thing a while back. Anyway, I did check it."

"And?"

"It's none of your business. Why are you so interested?"

"Reis's paternal grandfather was a jeweler and might have been the original owner of the picture. The timing is right. He and his wife were involved in a messy divorce. What if he, Carl Reis, wanted to hide money from the ex. He was a jeweler. He could've hidden jewels in the frame of his favorite picture. And then, what if she got mad and took the same picture never knowing what was hidden inside. Carl told both of his families he'd lost a treasure. But he never said what it was. Maybe Myrtle hid the picture in the basement of the clinic where she worked, which later became your diner."

"Sounds like you watch too many detective shows."

"Maybe, but it makes more sense than anything so far."

"There's nothing on the back but a hook."

"It would have to be hidden. Did you feel along the backing? Think about it. It wouldn't be too hard to hide several jewels, say diamonds, in a frame of that size."

Gus is silent for a moment. Then he says, "You're right. I felt something all along the inside edges. It was packed tightly."

"Oh my gosh, did you open it, Gus?"

Gus sighs, and when he speaks his voice cracks. "I did."

"And...," It occurs to me my eagerness to know is making Gus feel defensive and possibly suspicious. "I don't have to know what you found. But, it might explain the motive for all this violence. I encourage you to tell Detective Jones."

"Maybe I will."

"Would you like some help packing up?" I'm feeling hopeful Gus and I can reconnect.

"No, I can handle it. I'm sorry you've been hurt in so many ways. I wish you no ill will. Goodbye." He hangs up.

I sit there with the phone still up to my ear. I'm stunned. Hope of a reconciliation has died, I've lost Gus.

Chapter 29

After breakfast the next day, I continue my research. We need to know all the family members and their children. A few of the names sound familiar. I get out a list of people working in the police department. A chill runs down my spine. There are two cousins in the Shipley Police Department. One is a detective and the other is in the forensic department. This is what I've missed. Jessica's notes said she was going to check out the relatives. I've wasted so much time.

Suddenly my phone rings causing me to jump. It's Rob. He sounds rushed. "Suzanne, where's Gus?"

"He's working at the diner today packing it up for the sale. Rob, I know who the moles are."

"Who?"

"Forester and a guy named Meeks are cousins, and they're related to Reis. Meeks works in forensics."

"I'm at the emergency room, but it's nothing serious. Forester shot me. I was suspicious there was more than one mole, so I started watching the detective as well as the forensic guys. I got too close, and she spotted me. I ran, but she was still able to hit me. Nothing serious, she just winged me. I think she's going after Gus. Find him and warn him. I'll get there as soon as possible, and I'll bring help. Hurry."

It's like I'm moving in slow motion. Trying to gather my wits, I call Gus. There's no answer, so I leave a message. After hanging up, I begin to pace. He won't answer because he thinks I want to beg some more. He'll never suspect Forester. He needs to know now.

I run to the diner. Just as I get to the block of shops, I see flames shooting up in the back of Gus's Place. I approach the door, look over at the alley, and see Forester running out. She spots me and shoots. I fall through the doorway into the diner. I fear Forester might follow me, so I jump up and slam the door. A searing pain shoots through my left shoulder. I've been hit. Dazed and afraid to move, I see Forester at the door. For some reason, she doesn't come in. I keep waiting for her to shoot again. I duck down. I can't hear anything except noises in the kitchen from the fire. I'm terrified. Several seconds pass and nothing happens. What am I waiting for? I'm not dead. I need to find Gus.

Black smoke is rolling out of the kitchen making it impossible to see. I start to cough, drop to my knees, and slowly crawl towards the kitchen. Since the smoke is so thick, I feel my way across the floor using the bottom edge of the counter as a guide. I feel I'm not making any progress. I begin to panic. *Where's the end? Did I miss it?* Finally, I turn the corner and find Gus. He's sprawled face down behind the counter. I scoot up to his head to feel for a pulse in his neck and find a weak one. He's unconscious, but I can feel his breath. Rolling him over, I feel the front of his shirt is wet. I take off my jacket and press it down on his chest. He must've been shot, but there's not enough light to see where. I need to get him out of here before he bleeds to death or we both succumb to smoke inhalation.

I hear something that sounds like a loud bang in the kitchen. It's so hard to hear anything with the roar of the fire. I tell myself to keep going.

Gus is a large man at six feet and weighs around 220 pounds. I'm five foot two and weigh 105. I don't know where I will find the strength, but I have to save him. I move down to his feet and begin to drag and tug Gus around the corner of the counter. It feels like it's taking hours. I'm so hot and sweat is running into my eyes. I can feel the flames. I'm desperate to get us both out before we are burned alive. I'm terrified. He's too heavy for me. *I'm not going to make it. I can't fail him. I'm so sorry, Gus.*

Suddenly I feel a hand on my shoulder. Looking around, I find Rob. He motions me to go to Gus's head. He begins pulling his feet. He is moving slowly due to limited use of his arms. When we finally get to the front of the counter, I know from there to the door is thirty feet, but it might as well be ten miles. We slowly inch across a very hot floor. My arm is hurting and making it difficult to support Gus's head and push forward on his shoulders. I can't see anything. I pray we'll be able to get out of here. I will myself to stay conscious, as we struggle to drag Gus to safety. We keep stopping as we're both convulsed with constant coughing and my eyes are watering. I feel burning on my back but try to ignore it. I continuously repeat, "Keep going."

I lose all track of time, and I become convinced we won't make it. I feel myself giving up. *I'm so sorry, Gus . I failed you.* I can no longer see Rob. I can feel myself passing out. *Am I dying?* I lose consciousness.

Chapter 30

When I regain consciousness, I immediately feel around for Gus. He isn't there.

"Gus, where are you?" I try to yell, but it comes out as a croak.

A similar hoarse voice answers, "Suzanne, it's okay. You and Gus are in the hospital. You saved him. It's over."

***

I must have passed out again. When I open my eyes, I see Rob. He how has bandages covering his left shoulder and chest. His right arm is still in a sling from his previous injury.

"Is Gus okay?" I whisper.

"He's in surgery. He lost a lot of blood from the gunshot wound, but the doctor says he'll recover in time. "

"Thank God."

"Do you remember what happened?"

"It's a little fuzzy. The diner was on fire. I saw Forester run out of the alley as I reached the door. She shot me. There was smoke everywhere, but I found Gus. Then you arrived."

"You're amazing. You were shot, and you were still able to save Gus. You're a hero, Suzanne."

Detective Jones walks into the room. "I heartily agree, King. Thanks to the two of you, we got the moles and Reis."

"So, it was the cousins."

"Correct. Forester and Meeks were the moles. We were able to trace their contacts with one another. Meeks sabotaged the report and took the contents of the bag. Forester kept leaking Suzanne's whereabouts. And, she tried to frame me when she didn't go to the other safe house when I came to yours. And their cousin, Reis, is a real snake. He was playing both Jessica and Amy.

"These three couldn't wait to spill their guts. Each of them tried to get an immunity deal to sell out the other two. All three of them will be going away for a long time."

Rob asks, "But, what were they after? Those properties can't be so valuable they warrant murder."

"Those idiots felt they'd been shortchanged. They wanted their share of Carl Reis's riches, no matter who stood in the way. Apparently they'd been looking for some time before they decided it was in the tunnels."

Rob shakes his head. "So, no one knows what this so-called treasure really is or if it ever existed?"

"Reis has an old receipt for twenty five-carat diamonds. All three swear these jewels are buried in the tunnel. They claim they belong to their family. Amy must've realized Reis was using her to get to whatever he thought was down there. They argued when Reis revealed he wanted the tunnel dug up, and that was the end for Amy."

I shudder in disgust. "Animals. Why didn't they start digging once they killed Amy?"

Jones sighs. "They thought they had ample time to do their digging without being discovered. They wanted sole ownership of the entire tunnel. Then you and Gus found Bobby Rawlins, his bag from the bank robbery, and Amy's body. The sale got delayed. They seemed to panic. They thought you and Gus had found the diamonds. My guess is they then hatched the plot to frame you and Gus to get you out of the way. They couldn't risk someone finding their treasure."

I whisper, "How did Jessica figure into all this?"

"Reis found out Jessica was researching him and his family. He wined and dined her to find out how much she knew. Apparently she was on the right track, but she knew she had nothing to incriminate him or the others. He didn't believe her and had her killed."

"Did he hire Satchi and crew to terrorize all of us and hasten the sale?"

"Bingo. Reis revealed he met Satchi when he represented him in a robbery case several years ago. And ditto for the other shooters."

Rob shakes his head. "This is so unbelievable."

Jones responds, "Sad, but true."

I shake my head. "Hard to believe people get this crazy over money."

"This time around it was three people wanting what they thought belonged to them. They're a bunch of spoiled scumbags, if you ask me."

"Thanks for the updates, Detective Jones." I smile as I realize the bad guys are now gone.

241

"Yes, thanks, Jones." Rob has an equally big smile as he awkwardly shakes the detective's hand.

"You're welcome, but I couldn't have done it without you guys. You make a good team."

The detective leaves, and Rob resumes his seat next to my bed. I shift around a little trying to get comfortable. I'm beginning to realize gunshot wounds and burns are not fun.

"Do you need some pain meds?"

I shake my head as I readjust my position. "Not yet. I'm becoming aware of what happened to my body."

Rob grimaces. "An inch closer and you would've had a bullet in your neck. As it was, it missed any organs or arteries. What's that look?"

"I'm thinking about what Jones said."

Rob frowns. "What?"

"About the missing treasure."

"You want to go look for it?"

"No, I think it's already been found."

"What are you talking about?"

"I think Gus's father found it a long time ago." I proceed to tell Rob about the present Gus received from his father when they first got the diner. "His dad found this picture in the basement. It was under some moveable shelves left behind. Both Gus and his dad were huge Red's fans. So, they considered the find something special.

"Reis's grandparents came from Cincinnati. No doubt Carl Reis was a huge fan, too, of their hometown professional team. A picture of his team's first world series win would be a treasure to him. I can see a woman bent on hurting her ex-husband taking it away from him."

"I don't know where you're going with this. What does the picture have to do with it?"

"I believe there's more to the story."

"What do you mean?"

After swearing Rob to secrecy, I relate my conversation with Gus as to something hidden in the picture frame. I also tell him with Carl being a jeweler, there was good chance the hidden booty might be jewels.

"Where's the picture now?"

"Gus has it, and he's the only one who knows exactly what was hidden in the frame. At the diner, it used to hang above his desk. Please don't tell anyone."

"Of course not. Gus has been through enough. I wouldn't want to ruin this gift from his father. If it's jewels or whatever it is, it's going to the rightful owner, as far as I'm concerned."

"Thanks for understanding. I'm sorry, Rob, but I'm getting sleepy. I'll see you later." No sooner were the words out my mouth and I'm asleep.

I don't know how long I slept, when a nurse wakes me.

"Are you hungry? How about some supper?"

"Sounds good. I'm famished. How's Gus Breckman doing?"

243

She smiles and says, "I can't really talk about his condition, but I know your connection to him. Maybe you can see him tomorrow."

I eat most of my supper. Then I pass out again. When I wake up, it's morning. I don't know what's in this IV, but it must be strong. I feel like I ran a marathon. I look down to see Rob's head on my bed. I gently ruffle his curly hair.

"Are you finally awake?" Rob raises his head, yawns and stretches.

"Barely, but what're you doing here? You need your rest, too."

"Nowhere else I'd rather be."

"Now, Rob--"

"You can't possibly say you don't trust me after all this."

"Of course I trust you. You were a huge help."

"Jones thinks we're a good team. You heard him yourself."

I shake my head and readjust my position in bed. "But, I hired you. That means you were working for me."

He shrugs. "You never paid me."

"Send me your bill."

"Very funny, Suzanne. I'm crazy about you. We do make a good team."

I frown. "When the chips were down, you made me feel worthless. You don't treat someone you care about so cruelly."

"I was angry and scared for you. I wanted to stop you, so I tried to undermine your confidence. It was wrong. Instead of arguing with you, I should've offered to help. I screwed up, and I'm sorry. Please, please forgive me."

I sigh. "How can we ever make this work? I don't know anything about you. And, I've my own career and life to worry about."

"What have you been thinking will be your next venture?"

"Well, I want to stay in food service. I've been looking into my own catering business."

"What a great idea. I can help you."

I frown, feeling confused. "You're a private investigator."

Rob smiles as he shifts his sling higher on his shoulder. "I can change careers. I like to cook, and I could sell catering contracts."

"Wait a minute, do you want to work with me so you can boss me around?"

"Boss you? Impossible. You've convinced me. No one can control you. I'm proposing a business relationship, an equal partnership. Who knows where it will lead." He finishes with a flirty grin.

I return the smile, and say, "Hmmm...maybe we can work something out. We'll take it nice and slow, and see how it goes--" My statement is interrupted by his kiss.

About the author

Nancy Pflum was born and raised in Dayton, Ohio. She graduated from the University of Dayton with a degree in Secondary Education. She went on to Wright State University and earned a degree in counseling. She worked as a Clinical Counselor for twenty years and spent another ten years in real estate.

Nancy began writing in high school, but then came a long hiatus filled with raising two sons and having a career. Now retired, she has written her first novel, *Murder on the Menu.*

Nancy lives with her husband, Tony, in The Villages, Florida.

If you would like to give me feedback on this novel or find out about my new book, please send me a message.

storiesbyNancy@gmail.com

73489715R00141

Made in the USA
Middletown, DE
15 May 2018